The
Callahan Cousins

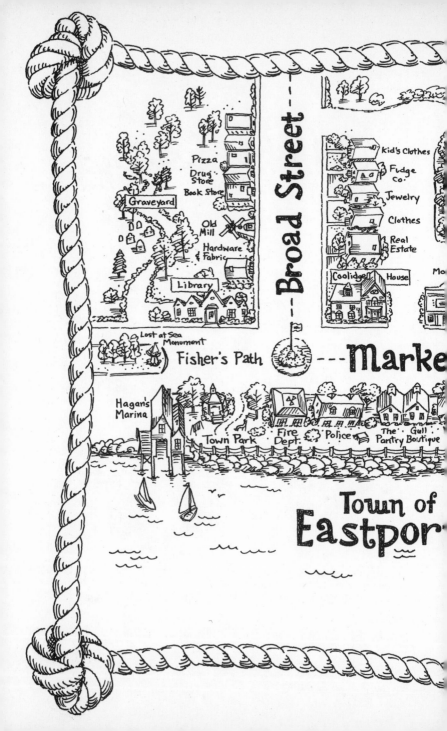

The Callahan Cousins

Summer Begins

by Elizabeth Doyle Carey

LITTLE, BROWN AND COMPANY

New York ~ Boston

Little, Brown and Company

Time Warner Book Group
1271 Avenue of the Americas, New York, NY 10020
Visit our Web site at www.lb-teens.com

First Edition: May 2005

Library of Congress Cataloging-in-Publication Data

Carey, Elizabeth Doyle.
Summer begins : a Callahan cousins novel / Elizabeth Doyle Carey. — 1st ed.
p.   cm.
Summary: Four girl cousins spend summer vacation together with their
grandmother on Gull Island.
ISBN 0-316-73690-2
[1. Cousins — Fiction.   2. Grandmothers — Fiction.   3. Islands — Fiction.]
I. Title.
PZ7.C2123Su   2005
[Fic] — dc22   2004016166

10 9 8 7 6 5 4 3 2 1

RRC

Printed in the United States of America

Book design by Alyssa Morris

The text was set in Mrs. Eaves and the display was set in Bickley Script

For Finn, Liam, and Alex,

with all of my love and gratitude.

May you have many happy times with your cousins!

Special thanks to Ayesha McFadden, David Ford, Ellen Jacob, Jennifer Hunt, Jodi Reamer, Lauren Levine, Maureen and David Egen, Pat Mahon, my sisters, sisters-in-law, and brothers-in-law, Tiffany Palmer, and all of my Doyle and Mahon cousins. And thank you most of all to the best grandparents in the world: Kathleen Doyle, William Doyle (in spirit), Richard Ravitch, Ward Carey, and Pat Carey. Were there ever luckier grandchildren?

"Send them to me," said grandma Gee.
And so they did.

CHAPTER ONE

Summer Begins

$\mathscr{T}$he late afternoon sunlight exploded off the waves in flashes and sparks, forcing Hillary Callahan to squint at the shore as her ferry pulled into the harbor. Gull Island rose out of the water ahead, as if waking from a nap to greet her, and the sight of it caused a warm flush of excitement on Hillary's face despite the cool June breeze. All around her, dotted across the water, were small islands of varying sizes. Hillary's eyes narrowed as she pored over the islands; clearly she was searching for one in particular. Just before they entered the harbor, Hillary caught a glimpse of the roof of The Sound, her grandmother's enormous shingled house on the northern tip of the island. And up ahead, at the southern end of the island, was Eastport Harbor, Gull Island's small (and only) town. Hillary scanned the old-time New England skyline of church spires and the tops of the low clapboard and brick buildings and breathed a small sigh of relief. Everything was just as she remembered it: the same, unlike the rest of her life back home.

Up ahead, clusters of people stood on the weathered wooden ferry dock, waiting to claim the boat's passengers and shepherd them to their final destinations on Gull Island. Hillary tried to make out the tall, lanky frame of her grandmother Gee, then craned her neck to see if any of her cousins were visible. Of course they changed so much from visit to visit, they'd be harder to spot, but she couldn't see little Neeve with her cowlicked black hair, or Kate's bouncy brown mane, or even Phoebe's bright blond hair that should have been shining like a beacon from the shore.

Phoebe, Kate, and Neeve ("It's Irish. It rhymes with Eve," Neeve always said briskly, sometimes even in her sleep), along with Hillary, had all been born in one year to four of the Callahan brothers. Among the twenty-six first cousins in the Callahan family, these particular cousins had always been friendly and enjoyed occasional weekend visits or holiday get-togethers, but they'd never spent any considerable period of time all together.

Now that they were finally twelve years old, it was time for their long-awaited "solo" stay at their grandmother's house on Gull Island — a whole summer without any parents! (Every cousin had a turn to do this once they were twelve; it was a family tradition.) So in they'd flown: Kate from Westchester County, just outside New York City; Phoebe from Florida; Neeve all the way from Singapore; and now Hillary from Colorado.

But as excited as Hillary was for her summer of relative freedom and time spent on Gull, she was still sad inside about the unraveling of her parents' marriage. This whole year had been a roller coaster of *Will they or won't they?*, and in the past month or so it had become clear that they probably would. Split up, that is. Done. Hillary couldn't believe it. When her father moved out and her mother changed back to her maiden name, Hillary felt like she was the only Callahan left in the world. She felt like her family had just disintegrated and she was desperate to hold on to any and all trappings of family life. It was essential for her to be with her dad's side of the family this summer and prove to herself that she was still close to them; still a Callahan. That was the main reason for the little project she had in mind for this summer. She could hardly wait to get the others alone so she could tell them.

"Oops!" said Hillary as she bumped into someone. Looking up, she realized it was the tall, preppy teenage guy she'd spied during the two-hour crossing.

"Excuse me," she said as a hot pink blush spread across her face. She always felt nervous talking to new people, especially boys.

"That's okay," said the young man, looking down at her with a grin. His chin-length blond hair kept blowing into his eyes and he pushed it away impatiently. "I can't make out the people who are meeting me either."

"Who are they?" asked Hillary, regaining some composure. "Maybe I know them." She forced herself not to be completely tongue-tied.

"The Bickets," said the young man, glancing back at the dock. "I'm coming here for the summer to teach sailing at Hagan's Marina and I'm living in the Bickets' garage apartment. I don't have a clue what the Bickets look like since I've only talked to them on the phone, but they said they'd be waving a yellow yachting flag."

Had he been looking at Hillary as he said this, he would have seen the surprise on her face. The Bickets! It was just too much of a coincidence! But she recovered quickly before he noticed.

"Oh, I don't actually *know* the Bickets, but I've heard of them, of course," said Hillary breezily, but inside her heart was pounding nervously. "Everyone has. They, um, they own the big grocery store here on the island." She quickly changed the subject. "I also know the Hagans! That's their marina, just to the left there. Some of my cousins have taken sailing lessons at Hagan's Marina in the past, and I think my grandmother said my other cousins and I will be doing it this summer, too. I've sailed before, just never here." She spoke quickly, hoping he wouldn't ask her anymore about the Bickets.

It worked. "Sounds like you have a lot of cousins!" Hillary nodded. "And hey, maybe I'll be your instructor at Hagan's. That would be cool," the young man said. "I'm Tucker Hill. What's your name?" He extended his right hand for a shake.

"Hillary. Hillary Callahan," said Hillary. *Shaking hands! How grown up,* she thought as she took Tucker's warm and calloused hand in hers. He was probably seventeen, but his earnestness and poise made him seem older. Hillary felt completely immature next to him. She felt a blush starting again and quickly looked back at the nearing dock to try to think of something else to say.

"Hey! There's a yellow flag!" Hillary pointed to a small cluster of people on the dock; one of them — a bored-looking dark-haired girl about Hillary's age — was lazily waving the flag in figure eights. Hillary was startled, though she didn't show it. She hadn't realized there was a Bicket girl who was her age. She studied the family carefully, sizing up the potential competition for her project. Other than the beautiful, pouty daughter, there were two parents who looked kind of normal, and a little boy who must've been the girl's brother. Tucker raised a hand in greeting but the Bickets didn't seem to see him; or at least none of them waved back. Just then, the ferry's engine shifted into a roaring idle as the captain began maneuvering the boat into its berth. A noxious cloud of diesel fuel filled the air, and Tucker said something Hillary couldn't hear.

"Pardon me?" she shouted.

"I said, I hope they're nice," Tucker shouted back.

"Oh, um, yeah. They're supposed to be, um, pretty nice. I'm sure it will be fine." But Hillary wasn't telling the truth. She gazed out over the water for a moment.

The Callahans and the Bickets had been on bad terms for years. Hillary didn't know all the details, but she knew that her dad and uncles had been friends with the Bicket brothers growing up, and then things turned sour. Over the years, she'd listened in as the grown-ups discussed the Bicket broth-ers and what jerks they had become. And her dad had told her time and again about a kind of wild, silly game that the Bicket brothers and Callahan brothers used to play — where family honor was at stake and winning a round meant winning one for the family and proving yourself a real Gull Islander.

Hillary's proposed summer project was to restart this game and win it once and for all. Over the course of the past few months, she had decided it was the only way to prove to herself and her dad that she was a true Callahan. And, even more im-portant, she figured it was a surefire way to prevent herself from being cut out of the family loop after the divorce. After all, no one would ever forget about the hero of their family. Would they?

Hillary snapped back to reality as the roaring of the ferry suddenly stopped. The captain had cut the engine, leaving only the noises of the gulls and the passengers' chatter, and the squeals of the boat against the wooden dock pilings.

Tucker smiled as he gathered up his huge duffel bag.

"Hey, it was nice to meet you." He slung the heavy bag up over one broad shoulder in a graceful arc and smiled at Hillary. "Do you need any help with your stuff before I take off?"

"No, thanks, that's really nice of you, but I'm fine." *The poor guy,* she thought. *From what I've heard,* he's *the one who might need help!*

"Okay, I'll see you when sailing clinic starts! Later!" Tucker called over his shoulder.

"Bye!" Hillary waved. "Good luck!" she added, but it was too late. He didn't hear her.

Tucker strolled off toward the front gate just as it opened, spilling the passengers onto the dock with its waiting throng of greeters. The cars on board the ferry began starting their motors, one after the other, as they waited to be waved off the boat by the deck hands.

Hillary shook her head slowly from side to side. *The Bickets,* she thought. *It's already starting!*

"Yoo hoo! Hillary!" Gee's voice rose above the crowd.

Gee! Hillary turned and spotted her grandmother at the far left of the dock. Gee hadn't changed at all since they'd seen her in Vail at Christmas. In fact, thought Hillary, Gee hadn't changed at all since before Hillary was even born. Her short, snow-white hair stood up all over her head like peaks of frosting on a lemon meringue pie. Her tan was as dark as ever, and her bright blue eyes — the Callahan family trademark — twinkled in dazzling competition with her wide grin. Gee was beautiful in an outdoorsy, healthy way, slim but well-muscled from her daily one-mile swim in the chilly waters of the sound (she was president of the local chapter of the Polar Bears Club, leading the charge into the water every New Year's Day) and energetic in her movements. And as always, she was beautifully dressed, right down to her usual pink lipstick.

"Hi, Gee!" called Hillary. "I'm coming around!"

Hillary hauled her mountaineering backpack into place on her shoulders, then looped between the cars on the ferry's deck and crossed through the boat's gate. She picked her way through the crowd and over to Gee, where she was instantly wrapped in an enormous hug that even encompassed the backpack.

"Look at you!" cried Gee, holding Hillary out at arm's length. "You're so grown up and lovely! Wait 'til the others see you. Of course they're all grown up and lovely, too."

Hillary laughed, thrilled to see Gee again, and relieved that Gee was the same as ever. Gee linked her arm through Hillary's to lead the way toward her ancient Volvo station wagon in the parking lot. They passed the Bickets, who were chatting with Tucker, and the dark-haired girl gave Hillary a cold, appraising look that sent a chill up her spine. Hillary stared back, sizing them up. Just then Tucker looked up and called "Bye, Hillary!" and Hillary waved. The Bicket girl's lip curled in displeasure and she turned her back to Hillary and looped her arm through Tucker's. Tucker seemed surprised but game as he gallantly led the girl toward the boardwalk to town.

The girl's father gave Gee a curt nod, and Hillary looked quickly at Gee to see how she'd respond. Gee nodded back cordially, ladylike and polite as ever. Although Gee had never been directly involved in any of the rivalry between her boys and the Bicket boys, she'd certainly heard plenty about it. She always said that she didn't approve of *anyone's* behavior in the whole thing, but she, too, had grown to dislike the Bickets over the years. She just wouldn't admit it.

It was weird for Hillary to see the always-friendly Gee looking so restrained; she could see Gee fighting her natural instinct to be friendly and chatty, while at the same time not wanting to be outright rude. Gee turned and smiled brightly at Hillary. "What a nice-looking young man that was with the Bickets! Was he on your boat?"

"Um, yes," said Hillary. She forced the Bickets out of her thoughts for the moment and said, "Tucker's his name. He's going to be an instructor at that sailing clinic we're doing. By the way, where *is* everyone? I thought they might come."

"Well, they're so excited that you're coming, they've been buzzing about getting things ready for you since they arrived two days ago. In fact, we just had a discussion at dinner last night about how they wouldn't feel complete until you'd arrived," said Gee.

"Really?" asked Hillary with a grin.

"Really! Now how was your trip?" asked Gee as they settled into the Volvo, Hillary's pack stowed safely in the back of the car.

"Not too bad," said Hillary. She gathered her long, salt-spray-dampened curls into a ponytail, crossed her legs in their olive green lowriders, then recounted her travels. Meanwhile, Gee steered the car out of the parking lot and turned left onto Market Street. To Hillary's right loomed the long and boxy Bicket Bouquet grocery store, but she purposely averted her eyes so she wouldn't have to see it.

Hillary looked out the window as they drove down Market Street, one of the lively harbor-town's two main shopping streets. Solid red brick buildings — the bank, the post office where you had to pick up your mail because they didn't deliver on the island — nestled snugly against white clapboard stores, virtually unchanged for over a hundred years. Her eyes combed the streets, checking for all her favorite landmarks. There was Booker's Sporting Goods, where Hillary had gotten her first soccer ball, and the News Co., where you could get piping hot cinnamon donuts with your newspaper every day. Across the street was Barefoot Toys, with the world's best collection of science stuff for kids, and The Dip, where their parents always took them for Awful-Awful ice creams ("They're awful big, and awful good!").

Where Market Street met Broad Street, there was a round-about, or rotary, instead of a stoplight. Hillary had always thought that was cool. They didn't have those back in Colorado. Here Market Street's name changed to Fisher's Path, and the Village Green with its Lost at Sea monument bisected it for about a block. The stores thinned out and neat little houses where the year-rounders lived clustered along the village lanes that led off Fisher's Path.

Hillary felt herself relax a bit more. *Gee's the same, Eastport Harbor's the same; so far, so good,* she thought. Nothing like home, where everything had changed.

"So what's new with the cousins?" asked Hillary.

"Oh, well, you're about to see for yourself, but personally, I think they're more themselves than ever before!" laughed Gee. "Phoebe's grown about a foot, and with that wonderful vocabulary of hers she seems about twenty years old. Kate has been needle-pointing and doing her watercolors, and baking wonderful things for us to eat. And Neeve. Good Lord! I don't know if her parents are doing the right thing, dragging those children all over creation, but she has certainly picked up some interesting clothing and habits from all those travels! I get such a kick out of the wild outfits she comes up with every day!"

Hillary smiled to herself. Nothing had changed with the cousins, either. That was good.

On the far side of town — just past the Cliff Church, with its rose-covered porch and Cabot's Clam Shack, *yum!* — Gee opened up the throttle and they started across the causeway. The sparkling navy blue sound extended out to their left, and to their right were farms and open fields; beyond them, on the eastern shore of the island, were the cliffs and then the open ocean. Hillary sighed and relaxed back into her seat for the short but scenic drive to The Sound. The air was so fresh and salty, and the sky so clear and blue that Hillary felt like her senses were being washed clean. She could feel the real world drifting away and the familiar island sensations and tempos begin to take hold.

"We're almost there!" said Gee brightly, startling Hillary from her thoughts. "Your spectacular solo summer is about to begin!" Hillary straightened in her seat and looked around. They were now in North Wing, the summer resort end of the island where all of the off-islanders had built their enormous summer vacation homes a century or so ago.

Just ahead was the final curve before the road dead-ended at the driveway to The Sound. White-shingled and black-shuttered, the rambling three-story "cottage" was the biggest house on the island; it simply teemed with cozy nooks, sleeping porches, unused passages, secret hiding spots, and over a dozen bedrooms and bathrooms. With its older central section, and two wings extending out from each side on a mild diagonal, the house looked like it was reaching out to hug you as you arrived. Hillary smiled as they passed the white painted name sign at the end of the driveway. CALLAHAN it said in black block letters. *You're darn right I am!* thought Hillary, and her smile widened into a broad grin.

CHAPTER TWO

Sound Sweet Sound

As the Volvo began its stately ride up the long driveway, the cousins were in the sunny, yellow kitchen at The Sound, where Kate was putting the final touches on the carrot cake she'd baked. Neeve, her tiny frame dressed in layers of shredded t-shirts and a skirt over a pair of painter's pants, was draped across the butcher-block island in the middle of the big, open room. She watched as Kate, round and cheerful in a pink polo shirt and khaki shorts, deftly piped the "-ary" of "Welcome Hillary!" in frosting on top of the cake.

Phoebe was lounging on the green-upholstered banquette in the breakfast nook trying to do the *Boston Globe* crossword puzzle, her long, thin legs stretched out before her in a pair of neatly patched old Levi's. Neeve had been teasing Phoebe that she dressed like a "hippie with a housekeeper," since Phoebe loved funky sixties clothes, but her natural perfectionism and neatness meant that they had to be pristine.

"I wonder if Hillary has been completely annihilated by her parents' separation," Phoebe said as she absentmindedly chewed on a pencil eraser.

Neeve threw a dishtowel across the kitchen at her and it landed on top of Phoebe's head. "Speak English, girl! You know I can't understand half of what you say!" Neeve's mild Irish accent became more pronounced when she was giddy.

Phoebe removed the dishtowel from her head with two fingers and, wrinkling her nose in distaste, placed it gingerly on the scrubbed wooden table. "Devastated. Ruined. Bummed beyond belief, if you insist on the slang." Phoebe dusted some imaginary crumbs off her spotlessly clean white embroidered peasant shirt.

"Ooh, I don't think so," said Kate, wide-eyed and earnest. "Hillary's so *brave,* always doing stuff on her own, going camping and doing experiments and things like that. I'm sure she's fine. Actually, I wish some of her bravery would rub off on me. I'm going to see if she can give me any tips this summer." She bustled across the terra-cotta tile floor to get more frosting from the bowl.

"Oh for Lord's sake!" interjected Neeve. "You can't get *tips* on how to be brave. You just have to do stuff! Anyway, you? Camping? Come on! At the first noise outside your tent you'd be hightailing it back to your minivan!"

"You're right!" Kate giggled, unaffected by the truth. "I'm a scaredy-cat."

Neeve took a swig of black coffee from her mug then wiped

her lips with the back of her hand. "Now hurry up!" she said, blowing her black bangs out of her eyes impatiently. "They're here!"

The girls could suddenly hear Gee's car tires crunching on the seashell-covered driveway. When a car arrived at The Sound it always sounded like someone was driving over bags of pretzels.

"Okay, okay," sighed Kate under her breath, as her dark eyebrows bunched together in concentration. "There! How does it look?" She stood back and licked a splotch of green frosting from her fingertip.

"Impeccable," declared Phoebe, who had risen to inspect Kate's handiwork.

Neeve groaned at Phoebe's word choice. "Let's go, smarty-pants! And you, too, Martha Stewart!"

"Go on now girls, I'll clean up." rasped a voice from the corner of the kitchen. The cousins all jumped. Sheila, Gee's ancient and strange Irish housekeeper, had just materialized in the pantry doorway. Her faded red hair was scraped back into a bun and her gaunt frame was wrapped in a gray cardigan, as if she was cold.

"Great! Thanks, Sheila!" said Kate as the girls dashed out of the kitchen, down the corridor, through the dining room and into the front hall.

Two car doors slammed in front of the house.

"Ready?" asked Neeve, grabbing the sign they'd made earlier under Kate's creative direction.

"You betcha!" cried Kate.

Neeve flung open the front door and shouted "Yo, Callahan!"

Hillary turned from the car's open tailgate and her face lit up with a huge grin. "Yo, Callahans!" she called, running towards the door. Gee smiled.

"Hi! Hi! Hi!" There was a flurry of hugs and kisses, punctuated by squeals of "You look *amazing*!" "No, *you* do!" Kate's sign lay on the front stoop where it had been tossed hastily aside. CALLAHAN GIRLS UNITED AGAIN! WELCOME HILLARY! it read. Hillary was thrilled to see them all, still looking the same, just a little older than last time.

"We are going to have *such* an excellent summer," pronounced Neeve.

"I'm so psyched to be here!" said Hillary.

"'Let the wild rumpus start!'" cried Phoebe, quoting from a book in her usual fashion.

"Yay!" Kate squealed in glee.

They were the same cousins, all right. Hillary smiled and turned back to the car. Gee had Hillary's backpack in her hand, but she shook her head when Hillary offered to carry it. Instead, Gee lowered it to the doorstep and spoke to them all at once.

"Now, I know your parents gave you all sorts of lectures before you came about how you shouldn't let me work too hard, or lift anything, or make me worry. But put that all out of your mind. I feel ten years younger with grandchildren in the house. I just want you to have a productive summer here: Be remarkable, and seize each day. And as your grandfather used to say: Don't give the house a bad name." Gee winked at them and they all smiled back. "But girls, really, most of all, be good friends to one another. Cousins last forever. Now, let's let Hillary freshen up and then you can all drag her off to do whatever it is you've been planning all day."

They trudged up the front steps and through the big green door, with the girls all talking a mile a minute.

". . . and then we need to go to town because you won't believe . . ."

". . . to the pool so I can show you this really cool new dive . . ."

". . . upstairs and we're right across the hall . . ."

Sheila was standing in the doorway to the back hall leading to the kitchen, wiping her hands on her apron.

"Hi Sheila!" cried Hillary.

"Well, the gang is all here," she said with a dry chuckle. "It's good to see you."

"You, too!" Hillary shrugged helplessly as the others pulled her along up the stairs.

Gee shook her head and laughed at them. "Hillary, you're not in your usual room. The girls will show you where you're all staying. Holler if you need anything. I'm just going to step out of the way here so I don't get mowed down!"

"Thanks, Gee!" called Hillary over her shoulder as the cousins spirited her and her backpack away.

Hillary barely had a moment to glance around before

Neeve had grabbed a t-back racing bathing suit out of the backpack and thrust it at her. Hillary shrugged gamely and ran to put it on, then they all skipped right back downstairs and through the French doors in the living room to the terrace out back.

"Oh!" said Hillary as she paused to take in the beauty of the grounds. There was the graceful green sweep of side lawn that bordered the house, and then the backyard, a rather run-of-the-mill term for the dramatic hillside that stepped gracefully down to a calm cove below. Thick, buttery shafts of sunlight poured through the tall treetops, and the air smelled the same as always: like a mixture of briny marsh and sweet, newly mown grass. "I always think that my memory of this is exaggerated, but it's the opposite! It's even more incredible than I remembered! And, *wow!*, how great to be at a house with our own pool!"

Running along the rear of the house was a sunsplashed brick terrace, where white iron patio furniture was topped with slightly faded pink-and-white-flowered cushions; down a level was another brick terrace with the rectangular swimming pool, comfy lounge chairs, and huge round planters full of pale pink geraniums. And nestled along the tree-ringed perimeter of the property were an underused grass tennis court, an herb garden, a trampoline, and a tiny pebbly beach, with a dock thrust far out into the water. Down to the left, behind a high hedge, was the Dorm, an old barn-like guesthouse where the teenaged cousins stayed when they visited.

Nothing at The Sound had changed since Hillary's last visit

two years earlier. Even the view was the same. Out in the distance, the water was dotted with chunky islets of all sizes — fifty-six of them to be exact, including Elephant Rock a hundred yards offshore (Gee's rule was that you had to be at least thirteen years old to swim to it) — and a handful of boats moved purposefully across this rocky blue canvas. Hillary stared at the islands for a moment, lost in thought. But this wasn't the moment to announce her plan. She'd tell them tonight, when they'd really be able to focus. She turned from the view.

"Shark, anyone?" shouted Hillary, as she scampered toward the pool.

"Ooh, Shark!" squealed Kate. "That game *petrifies* me! I love it but I hate it all at once because it's so nerve-wracking!" She clapped her hands together and gave a little jump of enthusiasm, then she and the others ran to catch up with Hillary. And one by one they all plunged into the pool.

CHAPTER THREE

We're Not Whingers

The girls sprawled on the beds and chairs in Neeve and Kate's room, completely wiped out by the swimming. Hillary couldn't decide whether to go unpack, or launch into telling the others her plan for the summer. She felt too tired for either at the moment. After all of the water games — Marco Polo, Shark, underwater tea parties, and breath-holding contests — the girls had dried off, jumped on the trampoline for a while, then returned to the house to veg before dinner. They'd now exhausted all the gossip on their various siblings and certain cousins (with up-to-date reporting on who had gotten a nose pierce, who'd passed their driver's test, and more), and burned through a discussion of all their favorite television shows, movies, and bands. The only thing left unmentioned was Hillary's situation at home. No one wanted to be the first to bring it up.

Hillary, nestled in a deep, comfy armchair by the window, was admiring how Neeve and Kate had each set up their own little areas. To Hillary's right, despite Phoebe having flung herself across it, Kate's bed looked cozy and inviting. It had a pale blue mohair blanket folded in a fluffy pile at its foot, and at the head Kate was leaning against a jumble of old, lacy baby pillows collected from Gee's extensive linen closet. Kate had draped her bedside table with a length of pink rose-printed vintage fabric from one of the attics and topped it off with a vase full of perfect pink roses she'd cut from Gee's garden.

Kate was busy needle-pointing a belt that had all the New York sports teams' logos on it.

"What are you making, Katie?" asked Hillary.

"Oh, it's for Ned's eighteenth birthday. Do you like it?" she held it up for Hillary to see.

"Yeah! Would you do one for me? Like with something else on it?" asked Hillary.

"Sure. I already made some for Julie and Brooks, and since they're so small, it only took me, like, a week for each one. But I did a backgammon board for my mom and dad's anniversary this year, and that was a killer. It took forever!" Kate was running on, so she didn't immediately notice Phoebe staring daggers at her, but Hillary did. She smiled. She knew Phoebe was trying to stop Kate from talking about parents and anniversaries or anything else that might upset Hillary. Finally Kate caught on. "Oh, I mean . . . I'm sorry . . ." she looked helplessly back and forth between Phoebe and Hillary.

But Neeve jumped in to change the subject. "Hey, Kate, would you make me one with, um . . . shamrocks on it?" Neeve asked. Hillary laughed out loud. Neeve hated touristy Irish stuff, but she was so desperate to avoid getting Hillary upset that she'd said the first thing that came to her mind.

"What?" asked Neeve innocently.

"Nothing." Hillary smiled. "I just thought you hated all that phony Irish stuff."

"Yeah, well, I've been away for a while. Maybe I'm getting sentimental," said Neeve, her eyes drifting back down to the Japanese comic book she was reading (in Japanese, of course).

Neeve's mother was from Ireland. Her parents had met and married when her dad, who worked in the U.S. Foreign Service, got his first diplomatic assignment to Dublin. They had lived in Dublin until Neeve was eight, her sister Ava was four, and her brother Frank was two, but Neeve still considered herself mostly Irish. After all, she had an Irish passport as well as an American one. All of this explained why Neeve's side of the room was dominated by a huge green, white, and orange Republic of Ireland soccer team banner that she'd hung on the wall.

"Maybe I should make you one with some kind of African design on it. Or Chinese characters?" suggested Kate, getting excited by the creative possibilities. Neeve's family had lived in Kenya after Ireland, until it got too dangerous, and then Shanghai, China, for a year. They'd been in Singapore for two years now, and by all accounts, Neeve was hoping they'd stay. "Chinese characters would be really cool, but you'd have to write it out for me first," continued Kate.

Phoebe snorted. "That's for sure. Otherwise Neeve would end up with a belt that said something like *Welcome, happy gum clock soda!*"

Everyone laughed, especially Neeve. Somewhere along the way, after their swim, Neeve had stuck brightly colored parrot feathers behind each ear, and there they remained, looking happy and festive.

Neeve was eccentric, all right, thought Hillary affectionately. But somehow, it all worked. She was filled with admiration for her cousin's ability to create little cocoons for herself, especially with such style and originality. Currently, Neeve's bed was covered in an outrageous orange, red, and yellow batik cloth from Kenya. Her bedside table displayed a Hello Kitty alarm clock (from spring break in Taiwan), a pagoda-shaped ceramic potpourri holder with a little bundle of fragrant orange blossoms and rose petals in it, an animal skin drum, and a handful of carved stone animals from Ireland that were her lucky charms. A sheer red scarf lay over her lampshade, casting a soft pinkish light. But the whole décor could change tomorrow, if Neeve had a new whim.

Hillary spoke up. "I bet you never ever get homesick, Neeve. You're so good at setting up your own little world wherever you go."

"Well, I don't know that I'm good at it — but there are things I need to do to get by. As much as I love to travel, I hate being new; I want to be local somewhere." Neeve twirled the jade worry beads she wore on a long cord around her neck. "I want a home base where I can walk through town and everyone knows me and my whole family. That's why I'm so psyched to be here for the whole summer and really dig in. I want Eastport Harbor to be my hometown . . . the place in the States that I can return to and really belong."

"Yeah, I know what you mean . . . ," said Hillary wistfully.

"But you *have* a hometown in the U.S.!" said Neeve.

"I know, but . . ." Hillary decided she might as well get the divorce talk over with. "I don't know if you guys have heard or not, but, um . . ."

"We've heard," Kate jumped in, her eyes large and round with concern. She was relieved that Hillary had finally brought it up herself. "We're so sorry and we just want you to know we're totally here for you, like if you want to cry or something."

"Yeah, and I could recommend some really good books for you to read, if you want. Like about kids whose parents are getting divorced. I've read lots. . . ." Phoebe shrugged helplessly.

Hillary felt a sudden urge to cry; more from gratitude, though, than sadness. One of the things that stunk about being an only child was that there weren't other kids in the family to talk to when things like divorce happened. Thank God for cousins.

"Oh, don't be so gloomy, you two!" interrupted Neeve impatiently. "Hillary is going to be fine. It's not like her parents are lost at sea, for Lord's sake. She'll still get to see them both all the time, right Hillary? C'mon! The Callahans aren't whingers or whiners, and we're here to have fun!"

Hillary laughed in surprise. Leave it to Neeve to change the whole tone of the room in one split second!

"What's a *win-jer*?" Kate was whispering to Phoebe.

"I think it's a British term for complainer. I could look it up . . . ," Phoebe offered in a low voice.

"Now. We've had enough of this lying around. Why don't we all just get changed and go down for some cheese and crackers before dinner?" Neeve stood up, and the others rose, too, buoyed along by her energy and decisiveness. Kate headed into the bathroom for a shower and Phoebe crossed the hall to the room that she and Hillary would share.

"You're fine, aren't you?" said Neeve quietly as Hillary made for the door.

"You know what? I think I actually am," said Hillary with a lopsided grin. "For now."

"Good. We'll just keep you really busy so you don't have any time to think about it," said Neeve briskly. She began opening drawers to search out the wild elements of her next ensemble.

"That's just what I was hoping," said Hillary.

Across the hall, Hillary and Phoebe's room was similar to Kate and Neeve's, but it looked east over the darkening front lawn rather than the sunset above the water out back. There were two twin beds, two bedside tables with lamps, two dressers, and a small cushioned window seat. Everything was immaculately neat, and Hillary's area was bare, save for her backpack with its contents gushing messily out of the top. Uh-oh. She'd forgotten what a neatnik Phoebe was. As an only child, Hillary had always had the luxury of her own room, and her slobby tendencies usually raged unchecked at home.

Phoebe's bed was neatly made with a patchwork crazy quilt as a bedspread and one of those big reading pillows on it — the kind with the arms and a pocket to hold your book. She also had a tiny reading light clipped to her headboard, and a small bumble bee bean bag perched neatly on top of the pillow.

Her bedside table was arranged with an exact row of identical picture frames. Hillary could just make out a pretty photo of Phoebe with her mom and dad and her two sisters back home in Florida (Daphne was sixteen and Melody was eight) and a picture of Phoebe's cat Frances, named for the author of her favorite book, *A Little Princess*. Every remaining square inch of the bedside table was covered in squared-off stacks of books. Many of them had a little bumble bee sticker on the spine; Hillary figured that must've been Phoebe's way of keeping track of which ones were her own, since her family nickname was Bee.

Hillary suddenly felt shy about unpacking all of her stuff in front of Phoebe. Also, it was weird to be alone, just the two of them. Phoebe was so studious and quiet that Hillary felt she had to think through what she said first; she couldn't just float along in the tide of Kate's constant chatter or ride the waves of Neeve's outrageous outbursts. Luckily, Phoebe spoke first.

"I can go first in the shower if you want, so you can have a little time to get organized."

"Thanks. That would be good," said Hillary gratefully.

Phoebe crossed the room to the bathroom, but she hovered awkwardly in the doorway for a moment. "I'm sorry I said the dumb thing about the books. And I, um, just wanted to add that my parents and I would really love it if you would come down and visit us this year. Y'know, get away from the cold and all that, and just relax."

Hillary smiled. "That would be fun. And don't worry about the book thing. I know you were only trying to help. It might be a good idea, anyway, in a few weeks. So thanks."

Phoebe paused for another minute. "Also, if you feel sad at night, like when you're going to sleep . . . I mean, sometimes at night I really miss my mom and dad when I'm away . . . anyway, you can always talk to me or wake me up or whatever." It was hard for Phoebe to talk about stuff like this; she was so reserved and formal usually, and Hillary was touched by the effort it was taking her to get the words out.

"Thanks, Bee. That's really nice."

"Okay, then. Shower." And Phoebe closed the bathroom door.

Hillary got to work, unpacking quickly. She wasn't a fashion person like Neeve, so she didn't have a lot of clothes. Most of what she'd brought was athletic gear — running shorts and shoes, fitted tank tops, some long-sleeved Nike and Reebok t-shirts, her Sweetie Sweats (okay, her one concession to fashion, but *everyone* wore them!) — and jeans. She stowed everything away in the dresser, then got to work on all the side compartments of the pack.

She pulled out her iPod, her lucky green bandanna, a tiny digital camera, a portable handheld microscope, a high-tech pedometer, and her *Skateboard* and *Snowboard* magazines. She randomly lumped them all onto the shelf under her bedside table. Next, she carefully unzipped the large padded compartment on the back of the pack and gently lifted her laptop computer out. Hillary was especially proud of this computer. It was as thin as a slice of bread and totally sleek, but it was quick as lightning and really powerful. She peeled away the bubble wrap she'd sheathed it in for the trip, and placed the computer gently on top of her bedside table.

Finally, she pulled out what looked like a lumpy, pinkish-gray rag. She quickly unfolded it and removed a framed picture of herself with her parents on vacation in Hawaii. It was the last time she could remember them being happy together, and she stared at it briefly, lost in thought. Then she quickly came to her senses and stowed the pink rag — the remains of her childhood blankie, named Pinky — inside her pillowcase so no one would see it. She placed the framed photo gently on her bedside table (*No whinging!*, she said to herself sternly) and turned as the bathroom door opened. Phoebe emerged, dripping, and Hillary was ready for her turn in the shower.

Moments later, with the hot water washing over her, Hillary pictured the reactions of the others when she announced her summer project. Her stomach flip-flopped nervously. She hoped they'd be as excited as she was. But she'd settle for just a willingness to participate.

CHAPTER FOUR

Two Against Two

By the time Hillary had finished dressing, the others had gone downstairs. She decided to have a quick snoop through the house before she went to the kitchen to meet up with them again. Besides wanting to stretch out a few more luxurious minutes of anticipation before she announced her project to the cousins, she also wanted to take a peek around to make sure everything in the house was still the same.

Hillary stepped out of her room and into the long hall that spanned the second floor of the house. It veered off at two angles from the central section. To the left was Gee's suite of rooms — her bedroom, dressing room, bathroom, and cozy little sitting room. Hillary could hear Gee inside, chatting on the phone and watching the news while she dressed for dinner.

Hillary took a right instead, so she could go down the back stairs. As she walked, she inhaled the smell of old, damp paint mingled with the clean odor of Murphy's Oil Soap. These twin aromas floated above an underlying salty dampness, and another, unidentifiable smell that was just Gee's house. Old wood or mildew perhaps. Whatever it was, it smelled heavenly to Hillary. *Eau de Callahan,* she thought, giggling. Familiar and promising, both.

As the central hall turned into the back hall, the family gallery began. All along the wall, in a chronological order that started with her own great-grandparents, Gee had hung scores of family photographs. Formal, sepia portraits became posed black-and-white shots, then more casual and jaunty snapshots. Some of them were hilarious, and it was especially weird for Hillary to see photos of her dad doing things on Gull that she still did — like eating an ice-cream cone outside The Dip, or diving into Gee's pool. The settings hadn't changed but the photos of him looked *so* old. It was like time travel.

Moving toward the end of the back hall, Hillary glanced into the familiar bedrooms along the way (besides the eight of them and Gee's suite on this floor, there were six more little ones between the attics upstairs). Everything was spare and immaculate in the darkened rooms, and Hillary sniffed deeply as little wafts of lavender reached her nose from the sachets that Sheila used to guard against moths.

Sheila had been a part of The Sound for as long as Hillary could remember, and even some of her dad's childhood stories made mention of her. She wasn't particularly warm or fuzzy, thought Hillary, but she wasn't mean either; just really busy and not so chatty. Hillary had always been sort of scared of her, when she thought of her at all. But now for the first time, Hillary did wonder about Sheila. Why had she left Ireland? Was she lonely here? Did she have any family of her own?

Hillary reached the back stairs and suddenly, she couldn't stand to wait any longer to make her announcement. She had to find the others. So she tore down the winding back staircase and landed smack in the vestibule off the pantry where the soda and beer fridge was. She poked her head into the kitchen, which smelled like a heavenly batch of chicken curry, but no one was there. Not even Sheila. Hillary cocked her head and could vaguely hear the girls' laughing, now, from the other end of the house, and she suddenly felt left out.

She looped through the kitchen and raced through the endless passage to the front hall, passing a half-dozen rooms large and small. Finally, she reached the screened-in sun porch at the end of the house. Looking like a little cocktail party, the others were arranged in ladylike fashion on the white wicker furniture, with sodas and a platter of cheese and crackers before them.

"There you are!" shrieked Neeve, who was now dressed in a lavender tutu, two tank tops, and a pair of leggings. "We were beginning to think about getting a search party together!"

Hillary grinned sheepishly. "I had to do a tour. Y'know, make sure everything was the same."

"Oh, I *know!* I always do that when I get here," agreed Kate earnestly. "It has to be the same." Kate was wearing a floral wraparound skirt and a pink t-shirt. Phoebe wore pale green gauzy pants with tiny mirrors set around the cuffs, and a white cotton short-sleeved sweater.

Hillary looked around. "Wow! I feel underdressed!" She had on a clean pair of white jeans and a short, fitted black t-shirt with a turquoise skateboard logo on it.

"Oh, we just felt like dressing up in honor of your arrival. Anyway, your outfit's great," said Neeve.

Hillary knew she'd have only a few minutes, at most, before Gee arrived, and she wanted to quickly let the others in on her plan. It was time for the announcement.

"Guess what we're doing this summer?" she said casually, but inside she was bursting with excitement. She couldn't wait to see their reactions.

"Reading one hundred books?" suggested Phoebe.

"Not *you*, Bee-brain, *us*, she said!" Neeve snorted. "What?" she turned to Hillary with a gleam in her eye, game as always.

Hillary paused for dramatic effect. "We're planting the flag!"

Neeve's jaw dropped and Phoebe looked aghast. Kate was confused.

Neeve recovered first. *"Yes!,"* she said, pumping her fist in the air. Stacks of silver bracelets jingled on her wrist in enthusiasm.

"Uh, that's not really up my alley . . . ," stammered Phoebe.

"What are you *talking* about?" said Kate plaintively.

"Haven't you ever heard of planting the flag?" Hillary was

incredulous. "You know, that crazy, wild old game that our dads had with those Bicket guys, where they'd sail out to that little island — the one that was shaped like Gull — and plant a Callahan family flag on it? Then the Bicket guys would go and rip out our flag and plant their own? And back and forth? And they were always getting in trouble and stuff? Didn't your dad ever talk about that?"

"Nope. I've never heard anything about it. It sounds kind of . . ."

"Hilarious!" said Neeve and "Scary!" said Phoebe simultaneously.

Hillary laughed. "That's the spirit, Neeve!"

"I still don't really get it," said Kate.

"Okay," Hillary began patiently. "Have you ever heard of the Bickets?"

"I guess . . ." Kate looked unsure.

"They're that family on the island, you know, who own the grocery store? Anyway, our dads used to be friends with them when they were growing up here, in the summers. Then, like when they were teenagers, they started getting in a fight with them. I'm not sure why. But this kind of war started, about who was the better family and, like, who were the true Gull Islanders. So there was this little island offshore in the sound, and it was shaped just like Gull. And our dads planted a flag with their name on it on that little island. And they claimed it was theirs, and it was a symbol of being a true Gull Islander if your flag was planted there. Then the Bickets went and tore it out and planted their *own* flag there. And then it went back and forth for maybe a year or two, where they'd rip each other's flag out and plant their own. It became, like, who's the cooler family, or, like, braver family." Hillary paused to take a breath. "The true Gull family," she finished decisively.

"Why would you want to start all that up again?" Phoebe wondered.

" 'Cause it's fun! It's an adventure! And we'd be upholding the Callahan name for our generation, and generations to come." Hillary was resolute.

"What's fun about it?" whimpered Kate nervously. "I don't think that would be fun."

"But it *was* fun. There are all kinds of funny stories from it that my dad used to tell me. Like, they dressed up as pirates one time when they went out. And once they snuck out at night and did it, and Phoebe's dad got bitten on the toe by a lobster and it swelled up and they hid it from Gee, but she found out and got really mad. And once they put someone's underpants up on the Bickets' pole. And another time this seagull, like, fell in love with Neeve's dad on the island and wouldn't leave him alone. . . ." Hillary's eyes were shining with laughter and excitement. "It was just silly stuff, but fun. And we could make it fun again!"

"How?" asked Kate blankly.

"Well, you know, like rig up a cool boat all for ourselves. Explore the little islands around here. Have adventures, get supplies, be secretive, you know. It would kind of be like a little club. Like an explorers' club! And you have to be a Callahan cousin to be in it!" Hillary was wracking her brain, trying to come up with ways to persuade Kate to say yes.

"What do we need to do to start?" asked Neeve eagerly.

"Find some new cousins to help you!" wailed Phoebe. "Oh, I just know where this is going. Whenever you two get together, it's always something. You always get just out of *control*!" She was practically wringing her hands.

Hillary and Neeve cackled simultaneously, then Hillary grew serious. "We just need to get a boat, figure out which island it is, brush up on our sailing skills, find the flag, get out there and plant it!"

"Oh, *that's* all!" said Phoebe sarcastically.

"Yeah."

"I don't know, guys. I think I'm with Phoebe on this one. It just sounds so hard and so . . . dangerous or something." Kate was tentative, but Hillary knew if she could sway her, then they'd finally get Phoebe to come around, too. Because two against two just wouldn't work.

"Look, Kate, there'll be lots of little crafty projects for you to do — packing picnics and gathering supplies and stuff. And Bee, there'll be research . . ." Hillary dangled this tantalizingly in a teasing, singsong voice. "Lots of research . . ."

"We are totally doing it," said Neeve decisively. "So you two better just buck up and join in and make Hillary happy. After all," Neeve added shamelessly, "her whole family is falling apart, it's the least you can do!"

Hillary laughed in outrage. "Neeve! You of all people!"

"I know, I know, but I just thought I'd tug on their heart-strings a little. They're the sensitive ones."

It worked.

"Do you really need us to do this with you?" asked Kate seriously.

Hillary hesitated. She wanted to laugh at Neeve's audacity, but she figured she'd better play it straight since they'd nearly reeled Kate in.

"Yes," she said levelly, refusing to look at Neeve. "I really do."

"Oh for God's sake, you two!" said Phoebe in frustration.

"Yoo hoo! Girls!" Gee's voice floated in from the living room. "Do I hear someone taking the Lord's name in vain!"

"No!" called Phoebe.

Neeve feigned shock. "*Phoebe!* And lying about it, too!" she whispered with a smirk.

"Good." Gee appeared in the doorway. "It's time for dinner. I'm sorry I'm so late but I got waylaid by Mrs. Talmadge on the phone about the Health Clinic benefit, and since I'm on the board, she wanted to run every last detail past me. Lord, that woman can talk!"

"Uh-oh! Who's taking the Lord's name in vain now?!" teased Neeve.

Gee clapped her hand over her own mouth in mock horror. "Shame on me!" she said. "Come on in, Sheila's all set for us."

By unspoken agreement, the topic of planting the flag was put to rest for now. All the girls seemed to realize they shouldn't discuss it in front of Gee. At least not yet. But dinner was a lively and jolly affair, as Gee entertained them with stories about the island and its various characters, and the girls eased comfortably into their solo summer on Gull.

That night, Hillary found herself too exhausted to discuss the plan again with the others. It would just have to wait. She crawled under her covers, feeling for Pinky in her pillowcase, and was fast asleep well before Phoebe had even switched off her reading light.

CHAPTER FIVE

Orientation

$\mathcal{H}$illary awoke first the next day and lay quietly in her bed, listening to Phoebe's gentle snoring, enjoying the bright sunlight streaming through their windows, and feeling happy to be at The Sound. She started to hum a jiggy little tune aloud, waking up Phoebe accidentally on purpose.

"What time is it?" groaned Phoebe from across the room. She was not a morning person, although she probably could have been if she chose to read during the daytime instead of into the wee hours of the night. *We should really call her Bat instead of Bee,* Hillary thought to herself. She laughed aloud.

"How can you laugh in the morning?" Phoebe moaned. "It's just not civilized."

Hillary sat up. "C'mon Bat! Time to wake up!"

"Bat? Is this some other new plan of yours? To rename everyone?" Phoebe was pretending to be cranky but Hillary could tell it was just an act.

"Nope, just you!" said Hillary cheerfully, and she swung her legs over the edge of the bed, climbed out, and tiptoed across the hall to check on the others.

Soon enough, they were all dressed and in the kitchen, where the phone was ringing off the hook for Gee. Gee's phone rang incessantly with calls from friends near and far, requesting her presence at teas, dinners or luncheons, or her help with fundraising, or a donation for a tag sale for the library. Since Gee was fun *and* organized, everyone who knew her wanted her involvement in their endeavors and festivities, one way or an-other. This morning, Sheila took messages since Gee wasn't there — she had gone for her swim in the sound and then to early mass at the Cliff Church, as she did every morning (she claimed it was because she had so many people to pray for, but Hillary's dad always said she did it because it was her only chance to be alone all day).

The girls had a hasty breakfast, choosing cereal instead of the full-cooked meal that Sheila offered to prepare for them. Sheila sniffed in disapproval of their choice, and expressed horror for the umpteenth time that Neeve drank black coffee.

She stood above the table, reluctantly refilling Neeve's mug. "What do yas have cooked up for today?" she asked.

Neeve swallowed a mouthful of Lucky Charms; she could never get enough of the junky American cereals whenever she was back in the States. "Not much. Some errands. Some *flag planting.*"

The others were shocked Neeve had said something about it, but Sheila practically jumped out of her skin. The coffee sloshed in the pot until she steadied her hand.

"Now why would yas go doing a thing like that?" she asked breathlessly.

Hillary thought Sheila's reaction was a little extreme, but she didn't have time to wonder why. She just needed to cover up for Neeve's big mouth.

"She's just joking, Sheila. We're doing nothing of the sort," said Hillary, kicking Neeve under the table.

"Ow!" cried Neeve with absolutely no tact. But Phoebe glared at her and she shut right up.

"Good. I wouldn't want to hear of that can a'worms opening up again, I can tell yas that. And yer grandmother sure wouldn't like it one bit. She doesn't like conflict and that's one that was finally laid to rest. Better left that way." Sheila seemed to have recovered and she crossed the kitchen to replace the coffee pot on its burner.

Kate, ever the peacemaker, spoke up. "Yeah. We won't mention it ever again, Sheila. And maybe you'd better not tell her that Neeve was even joking about it, okay?" She, too, stared daggers at Neeve. Neeve looked uncharacteristically chastened for once.

"I'd never," said Sheila.

Outside, in the cavernous shingled garage, the girls berated Neeve for being so careless.

"I was just joking around!" she wailed. "How was I supposed to know she'd have any idea what it meant?"

"Loose lips sink ships!" said Phoebe sternly.

"Alright, I think Neeve has gotten our point," said Kate. "Let's all just be nice."

But Hillary was secretly pleased by the incident. They were treating the flag-planting plan like it was a fact, and they were all in on it.

"So . . . ," she ventured cautiously, "it sounds like you guys are in?" She looked from Phoebe to Kate to gauge their reactions.

Phoebe flipped her hair. "I haven't decided," she said breezily.

"Me neither," added Kate meekly.

"Well we need to know today. There's no time to waste," said Neeve firmly.

"We'll think about it," Phoebe said, and Kate nodded.

Hillary sighed. She hated to wait.

The girls had planned to ride bikes to town to do errands, and Gee had left them a note asking them to go to Hagan's Marina to register for sailing clinic. In Gee's garage were a dozen or so old bicycles that had been spray-painted entirely red so that they'd be impossible to lose. Any red bike in town was recognized as a Callahan bike by all. So the girls each grabbed a red bike — careful to pick the ones with baskets big enough to accommodate any purchases — and they set off for town.

Everyone's parents had given them a hefty allowance for the summer; not that they were expected to spend it all, but because the girls had been instructed not to ask Gee for money. Yet everyone knew this was a joke; money practically *bled* out of Gee's pockets — especially when there were grandchildren around. She was always peeling off cash or diving for the bill in restaurants. She hated to think of others paying for her or anyone in her family, and she was horrified by the idea that a child staying at her house might not be able to buy exactly what he or she wanted whenever he or she wanted it. Therefore, she left fifty dollars apiece for the girls on the counter every week. If they didn't spend it, they just saved it for a "rainy day." There was no way to refuse Gee; you just had to take the money and shut up.

The girls had decided to have their annual Pig-Out that night, so they needed to stock up on junk food. The Pig-Out was a ritual they always had every time they got together and it involved buying and then eating as many kinds of junky sweets as possible; half the fun was just gathering up the stuff for it. Afterward, they always felt sick, but it was worth it for the laughs along the way.

Their first stop on the way to town was The Little Store, a small general store, crammed to the rafters with household staples, beach gear, newspapers, and most important of all, penny candy. It was the only store on the North Wing of the island, so Gee often sent grandchildren there to pick up things she had forgotten to buy in town. She would also send them sometimes — just to get them out of her hair for a while — with a dollar bill each, instructing them to see who could buy the most penny candy with their money. The girls ditched their bikes in the rack outside and piled through the doorway, its little bell tinkling in announcement of their arrival.

Inside, large wooden barrels of sunscreen, beachballs, and assorted summer necessities were lined up like sentries in front of the counter. On the opposite wall, the wooden shelves bore heavy loads of penny candy in lidded glass jars, and old-fashioned general store–type shelving stretched to the back of the store in two small aisles, offering everything from island-style gifts to couscous and bug repellent. Beach chairs, buckets, and coolers hung from the ceiling, making the most of the small space.

The store's proprietor looked up at them from her perch behind the counter and smiled warmly. She was a heavyset woman in her thirties, beautiful in a weather-beaten way, with flyaway blond hair pinned up in a clip. Dressed in a flowing, batik-print hippie dress and long dangly earrings, she was reading a book titled *Woman Warrior: Maximize Your Inner Power,* which she set facedown on the counter so she could focus on the girls.

"Well if it isn't the Callahan girls!" said the woman in greeting. Her voice was surprisingly girlish and pretty.

"Hi!" said the girls in unison, caught off-guard by her friendliness as well as her knowledge of who they were.

"I'm Farren," she said by way of explanation. "Your grandmother has been so nice to me since I bought the store last fall, and she's been so excited about your arrival. I feel like I know you already!"

"Oh, right, she told us about you last night," said Neeve, who was the most comfortable with meeting new adults. The other three girls felt a little shy. "I'm Neeve, this is Phoebe, and Kate, and that's Hillary." Hillary blushed when Neeve pointed her out, but it was plain to see how Neeve herself just lit up with excitement when she met new people.

"Welcome to Gull! Holy moly, you all look a lot alike, now that I really look at you. Especially those blue eyes. You've all got 'em, you lucky devils! Strong genes," said Farren. "So how long are you here for?"

"The whole summer!" replied Neeve enthusiastically. "Every time someone in our family turns twelve, they get to come spend the summer at Gee's without any parents!"

"Wow! That's so cool!" said Farren. "What do you do while you're here?"

The girls filled her in on their plans, including sailing clinic, lots of beach time and movies, and the Pig-Out. No one mentioned planting the flag. Hillary half-hoped that Kate or Phoebe would say something, but they didn't and she felt a little let down.

"It's all very exciting, isn't it?" said Farren. "A summer on your own on an island. Independent young women! Adventure! Staking your claim!" She had a dreamy expression on her face now.

Ooh! thought Hillary, brightening. *She's kind of nutty, but she might be a mind reader!*

"Well, keep me posted and let me know if you need anything. I love adventures!" Farren was saying.

The girls spread out to make their candy selections, and soon they each had a white paper bag bulging with treats. After they paid, Farren walked them to the door to see them off. "Good luck and Godspeed, as they used to say around these parts. And remember, *A journey of a thousand miles begins with one step!* Peace." Then she went back inside, the bells around her ankle jingling in unison with the bells on the door.

Outside, the salt air was so clean and cool that it felt sharp inside Hillary's nose. Few cars passed as they rode to town, and with the calm blue water to her right and the open fields and farmland to her left, Hillary could imagine what this island must have been like a hundred years ago when her great-great-grandfather first came on a dare, after a long night out with a group of friends. Talk about a deserted island! A few fishing shacks, a boarding house, and a pub. That was all.

Their next stop was two miles up Fisher's Path at Hagan's Marina, the A-frame cedar building that was the headquarters of the local sailing school. Mrs. Hagan — with her steel gray bobbed hair, tanned and wrinkled face, and perennial slash of white zinc oxide across her lower lip — cheerfully registered the girls for their classes and handed them their gear lists and some permission forms for Gee to sign. Gee had told the girls at dinner last night that they'd need lots of new gear for sailing and had instructed them to head over to Booker's Sporting Goods in town and charge the stuff on her account. Hillary was excited. She loved gear.

The rest of the morning they spent wandering around town. Phoebe wanted to get her own library card and see if the library had up-to-date sea maps and stuff, "Just in case," she'd said in an exaggeratedly put-upon voice. But Hillary could tell she was secretly eager to get started on some research. That was a good sign.

The girls dropped Phoebe off first, since the library was just past the Village Green, across the street from Hagan's. The Gull Island Public Library was a rambling, old one-story building, but its tiled roof swooped up to peaks and dipped down to gullies and gave it the appearance of a wacky castle for a modest queen. Phoebe said it reminded her of the house in the old movie *Bedknobs and Broomsticks,* with the building stretching out in weird directions and the roof poking up all over the place. She waved happily as she shoved her red bike in the rack outside, and the others went on, promising to meet up for lunch at noon.

A little farther into town, the three girls made a left on Broad Street. Their next stop was the Old Mill — a crafts store housed inside a shingled antique windmill about halfway down the street. Inside, Hillary looked around for a bit at the shelves stretching up the thirty-foot-high circular interior.

She watched the saleswoman expertly drag a very tall ladder on a track around the wall, and then lightly scale it to retrieve things for customers to inspect. Hillary loved heights, but her palms began to sweat nervously just from watching the sales-woman. Or maybe it was from being surrounded by so many sequins, ribbons, and paints. Crafts were definitely not Hillary's thing — she didn't have the patience for them and she always preferred to be outside running around rather than indoors and seated. So while Neeve stocked up on zillions of tiny beads for making bracelets, and Kate examined rainbow-hued tubes of paint and thick watercolor paper, Hillary hastily said her good-byes and slipped out the door. She'd meet them at Callie's Cupboard at noon for lunch.

Hillary was actually grateful for a little time alone as she am-bled along the tree-lined shade of Broad Street. As an only child she was used to her privacy and she found it a tiny bit tir-ing to be with other people this much. Plus Phoebe and Kate moved at a much slower pace than Hillary liked to; she some-times felt like a dog on a leash when she was with them, as if she was being held back from romping and running free.

The first thing Hillary did was cross the street to stop at the Fudge Company to buy the essential Gull Island treats for the Pig-Out: saltwater taffy and some peanut butter fudge. Then she strolled along, window shopping and nibbling at the fudge (just to make sure it was up to snuff, of course). She passed real estate offices, and little jewelry boutiques with delicate necklaces laid out on velvet in their windows. She peered into the windows of clothing stores that sold all manner of summer necessities and luxuries, from bikinis and sarongs to sturdy red twill pants and whale-printed corduroys. These were the places her mom always liked to stop and shop when she was here, thought Hillary. The sudden lump that rose in Hillary's throat made it hard to swallow the fudge, so she stuffed it back in the bag and walked on. Hillary's favorite places were on Market Street, and she quickened her pace in anticipation.

When Hillary reached the corner, where the fancy and formidable red brick Coolidge House hotel stood, as it had for over ninety years, she turned left onto Market Street, which ran parallel to the shoreline. The movie theater was showing two movies — one classic and one new, as usual. Right next door, the gleaming plate-glass window of The Dip invited strollers in for an ice cream at its long, old-fashioned soda fountain counter. She passed Gull Vibe, a music store selling CDs and movies, and poked her head into Barefoot Toys to see what was new in there; then she crossed the street to inspect the earring studs in the window of Gullboutique. Hillary's mom had talked Hillary's dad into letting her get her ears pierced there three summers ago. Her dad had argued that pierced ears on a nine-year old were tacky, but her mom had said something about women's rights and the importance of Hillary learning how to take care of her own body, and she'd won the argument, delivering the good news to Hillary with a conspiratorial wink. Hillary smiled, thinking back on it.

Outside the News Co., Hillary took a huge gulp of cinnamon-donut air and dashed inside to stock up for the Pig-Out. The Callahans were big fans of these donuts; her dad always got them in the morning when he was here, and just smelling them made Hillary ache a little with homesickness for him. She paused at the Pillar outside the News Co. to read the notices. Babysitters wanted, pets lost, knitting lessons, houses for rent, the usual. She moved on, ambling past the assortment of junk stores full of tourist stuff that took over this side of the street as she got closer to the docks. These stores' names might change from year to year, but the stuff they sold never did — bumper stickers, fake scrimshaw, fancy shells, t-shirts, pukka beads, flip-flops, and boogie boards — stuff her parents always teased her for buying.

Visiting all her local haunts, Hillary was comforted by the sameness of Eastport Harbor, but also sad that her mom and dad weren't with her. She missed them and felt sick suddenly when she realized her mom would probably never come here again.

Hillary nearly jumped out of her skin as the noon whistle blasted. Every day at twelve o'clock on the dot, the fire department blew its ear-splitting siren, presumably to let everyone know it was lunchtime — or that the siren still worked; Hillary wasn't sure. But she realized she was due to meet the others at Callie's Cupboard for lunch right then, so she hustled on down Market Street. Maybe Kate and Phoebe had made up their minds. She couldn't wait to find out!

Hillary strode athletically toward the delicatessen, absent-mindedly looking at the stores along the waterfront, glimpsing flashes of the sound beyond them as she passed. She felt a kick of excitement as she saw the others waiting for her outside, and she quickened her pace and hurried to meet them, anxious for a decision. But as she drew near, she could see Neeve shaking her head slowly from side to side. Hillary slowed down and sighed. Kate and Phoebe were killing her.

CHAPTER SIX

Frozen

Booker's Sporting Goods had expanded and been given a facelift since Hillary's last visit — one of those rare changes for the better, thought Hillary. During lunch, Hillary had wrestled with her disappointment over Phoebe and Kate's reluctance, and had finally convinced herself to be patient for a little bit longer. By the time they arrived at Booker's, Hillary was excited again and her head spun from surveying the store's dizzying new array of supplies. They had a huge section for sailors, a giant "Boarder's Corner" for snowboarders, surfers, and skateboarders, plus smaller areas for runners, swimmers, climbers, skiers, rowers, and even a tiny triathlon section! The salespeople were excited to help such enthusiastic customers with their purchases, and by the end of the spree, there were four big stacks of sailing stuff — foul-weather gear, canvas tote bags, rubber-soled shoes, polarized sunglasses, compasses, sailing knives, and more — on the counter and everyone was laughing and having fun, even Mr. Booker, who'd come down from his office to see what all the hoopla was about.

Neeve had been flirting madly with the sales guy who helped her — a strikingly gorgeous fourteen-year-old named Talbot, who had grown up in Jamaica and recently moved to Gull full-time with his family. He was tall and gangly, like any teenage boy who'd just had a growth spurt, but his mahogany-brown skin, island accent, tiny dreadlocks, and high cheekbones made him seem more like a Gap model than an awkward teenager. His knowledge of sailing and the sea in general also made him seem older, but he admitted that he'd just picked up a lot of information from his dad, who was a commercial fisherman. His expertise was surfing, he said, which Hillary could've guessed from his long shorts, rash-guard turtleneck, and California beach lingo. He talked like someone from a teen surfer movie.

Right before the four cousins left the store, Neeve stood on her tiptoes and pointed to a row of braided white rope bracelets hanging behind the counter. "We'll also take four of those, please. I'll pay for them myself." Talbot handed Neeve her small package, and she tucked it inside her tote bag, which was so huge it made her look like an elf carrying Santa's pack.

With their transactions finished, Talbot seemed reluctant for them to go. "So Callahans, yo, if you ever need anything, or anyone to show you around the island, you know . . . I'm your guy!" said Talbot with a huge grin. Phoebe elbowed Kate and raised her eyebrows knowingly, then they both giggled. Talbot had a crush on Neeve.

"Thanks!" said Neeve, cool as a cucumber. But then her eyes narrowed as she had an idea. "Actually . . . since you seem to know a lot about the waters around here, do you think you might be able to help us out? We're kind of on this quest — it's a long story, but we need to get to one of the little islands and we're not so familiar with sailing on our own around here."

Hillary felt a leap of excitement in her chest. *Go Neeve!*, she thought. *Way to keep the ball rolling!* She glanced at Phoebe and Kate to see what they thought of Neeve's request. Phoebe looked pained and Kate seemed vaguely nauseated. Hillary laughed. "We'll get you yet!" she whispered.

Talbot nodded. "Sounds rad. Yo, I have Thursdays off and I usually hang at Macaroni Beach with my buddies. Why don't you check it out around lunchtime and we can grab chow at The Snack and I'll see if I can help you."

"Brilliant!" cried Neeve. Hillary smiled. None of them would have had Neeve's smoothness in negotiating plans to see him again, let alone roping him into helping them. She was pleased that Neeve had handled it so well for them — and the other two seemed happy that they'd get to see Talbot again, despite their misgivings about the flag-planting plan.

Outside, the girls teased Neeve mercilessly about her new boyfriend, and with that accomplished, decided that they had to have ice cream right then or they'd die. So they jammed their stiff new tote bags into the bikes' baskets and quickly steered their way up the street.

It was a little slow inside The Dip, and the girls had the whole long, marble counter to themselves. They sat on high stools, swiveling from side to side and licking butterscotch sauce from the long metal spoons that came with the Awful-Awfuls.

"So how was the library, Bee? Did you find anything?" asked Hillary hopefully through a mouthful of marshmallow.

Phoebe placed her spoon on her saucer and formally folded her hands in her lap, looking like she was getting ready to deliver a report in school. She swiveled to face the others from her spot at the end of the row and, with a long-suffering look, explained what she'd found.

"All right, you know I'm still skeptical about this idea, but I did poke around the library a bit, and I introduced myself to the head librarian. They have all the up-to-date maps, or, what did she call them? Charts, of the islands surrounding Gull. I didn't get into detail about what we were looking for, but she said we could come back and she'd help us . . ."

Just then the bell above the door jingled and the girls turned to see who was coming in. Neeve looked relieved for the distraction from Phoebe's long-winded answer to their question.

It was Tucker.

"Hillary!" he cried, as if she were a long-lost friend. Hillary pinkened, but she was pleased to see him, too. He crossed the room in three long strides while the others looked at her, confused. Who was this guy? Hillary realized that in the excitement of her arrival yesterday she had neglected to tell them about the cute sailing instructor she'd met on the ferry.

"Hi, Tucker," she said with a smile. She felt a tiny bit pleased to have made a friend without the others' help — particularly Neeve's. Even though Neeve's social skills were a huge help for the group, Hillary could get a tiny bit tired of feeling like a follower after a while.

"And these must be the famous cousins!" The other three girls grinned, happy that he'd heard of their existence.

"Yes, um, this is Phoebe, Kate, and Neeve. And guys, uh, this is Tucker. He's going to be one of our sailing instructors at Hagan's." Hillary gestured awkwardly between them, making the introductions.

Phoebe smiled and shyly dipped her head, and Kate said hi. Neeve, of course, nearly lunged across the counter to shake his hand, and Hillary felt a tiny flicker of irritation at her.

"So you must be a big sailor, then, yourself?" said Neeve lightly.

Hillary was conflicted. On the one hand, it was annoying the way Neeve flirted with every guy she met. But at the same time, Neeve *was* at least trying to help Hillary's flag-planting cause. Hillary looked to Phoebe and Kate for some kind of help, but they just shrugged, as if to say *You started it.*

"But of course!" Tucker laughed and glanced around for a place to sit. The only open stool was at the end, next to Neeve, and he made his way down the counter to reach it. "Do you mind if I join you? I've got a little time to kill and I've heard this place is awesome."

"Actually, it would be grand if you joined us. We were just talking about a little sailing project we want to do, and maybe you could help us," said Neeve, smiling a dazzling smile at him.

Grand!, thought Hillary. *Neeve's really working the Irish accent.*

"Hey, are you Irish?" Tucker asked, and they were off and running on the topic of Neeve's fascinating background.

Inside, Hillary groaned, but Tucker didn't seem to mind Neeve's chattiness or her request for help. *He must be really lonely,* thought Hillary, *to seem so happy hanging out with a bunch of twelve-year-olds.*

But Tucker wasn't condescending or anything, and after he placed his order with the counter girl, he gave them his full attention.

"So what do you need to know?" he asked as he propped his long, khaki-clad legs on the footrest under his stool.

"Everything," muttered Phoebe.

Tucker smiled. "Do you guys know how to sail?"

"Hillary does," said Kate loyally. "She's really good. But the rest of us are . . ."

"Landlubbers," Phoebe offered drily.

"Speak for yourselves!" cried Neeve. "I've been in a boat or two in my day."

"Okay, then. Uh, let's see. It would be easier if we were actually in a boat, 'cause then I could think of stuff to tell you a little more easily. But, I guess the most important things about sailing are being safe and being prepared; they're really one and the same. Um, before you get into a boat, you want to make sure it's in ship shape: no leaks, no rips in the sail, functioning gear and tackle, a working anchor. All that. Do you have a boat?" he asked.

"Maybe," said Hillary, craning her neck past Kate and Neeve to answer the question. She knew Gee had always kept an old wooden sailboat for the grandchildren to tool around in, but she hadn't had a chance to look for it yet.

"Okay, well if I were you, I'd see if I could get an expert to do an inspection of it. Make sure it's seaworthy. I'm sure someone down at the boatyard could do it for you. They might even make a house call so you don't have to drag it down there on a trailer."

A trailer! House calls! Hillary bit her lip worriedly and pushed her hair behind her ears. There was no way they could do any of that without Gee finding out and asking all sorts of questions. Hmmm.

The others didn't glance around, so Hillary wasn't sure what they were thinking. Kate and Phoebe would of course be riveted by any safety information, and Neeve would be riveted by anything that came out of this cool older guy's mouth. They'd have to figure out the logistics later, then.

"Next," he continued, pausing to thank the girl for his ice cream and take a big bite. "You want to make sure all of your safety equipment is on board and in good shape. You'll need a bailer, some rope, extra life vests, a few flares, a couple of oars . . ."

"Oars? What for?" asked Kate in alarm.

"For if the wind dies down and you're stuck somewhere," said Tucker matter-of-factly. He took another bite. "Happens all the time with little boats, 'cause their sails are so small they don't pick up a lot of wind."

"Oh God . . . ," moaned Phoebe.

"Shush!" said Neeve brusquely. "What else?"

"Let's see . . . a few basic rules of conduct on boats: First of all, don't ever stand up in a small boat. They can be really tippy. Second of all, the captain is in charge at all times and the crew needs to work as a team."

"So we need to pick a captain . . . ," said Neeve thoughtfully.

Tucker took another enormous bite of his ice cream and they waited patiently to see what else he had to say. "Thirdly, you have to make sure to check the weather conditions before you go out in a boat. Also, Hillary, you probably know this from the times you've sailed before, it's always colder on the water than on land. So you should bring a sweater or windbreaker to wear under your life vest, or better yet, a wet suit."

"A wet suit!" cried Kate.

Hillary was pleased he'd singled her out for her sailing experience. But she also groaned inwardly. *This was not a good idea,* she thought. *He's just going to scare Kate and Phoebe off.*

"Yeah, well, if you fall overboard . . . it can help keep you from getting hypothermia. The water's really cold up here in New England."

"Great. Now I know for a *fact* that we're risking our lives!"

said Phoebe. She crossed her arms and set her mouth in a grim line.

"Don't worry," Tucker laughed. "I'm sure Hillary will make a great captain and nothing like that will ever happen."

Hillary nearly fell off her stool. *Captain?! Me?!* She looked around at the others but no one was protesting, so she didn't say anything.

Tucker had really warmed to his topic and he obviously knew a lot about sailing. *He's probably a really good teacher,* Hillary thought admiringly. He licked the last bit of ice cream from his spoon and continued. "Now, another key preparation is to let someone know your plans. Never leave a dock without telling someone exactly where you're going and what your planned route is, and your estimated time of return. This is crucial, especially out here on an island, where the tides and weather can turn quickly."

Neeve was surprisingly quiet for once, drinking in everything Tucker said. Hillary's mild annoyance with her melted into gratitude as she saw how seriously Neeve was taking this.

"And speaking of tides, you always want to make a note of the high tide and low tide times, because the way the water runs out here through the channel and the islands, you'll be affected by it. They have what's called a spring tide here, and if it's running . . ."

Suddenly the door to The Dip banged open. The girls turned to see what the racket was about and there was the Bicket girl Hillary had seen on the dock, but this time her hands were weighted down with grocery bags from the Bicket Bouquet. She had had to kick the door open with her foot to get in, and she did not look pleased. Her green eyes flashed and her long, rangy arms and legs radiated impatience.

"Tucker!" she called in a sharp voice. "What's the deal? I've been waiting for you for hours!" She gave the Callahans a frosty once-over but she didn't smile or say hello. She just stood, waiting for Tucker.

Tucker rose dutifully and crossed the room to relieve her of her burdens. He looked at his watch when he reached her. "Hello, Sloan. It couldn't have been hours, 'cause I've only been here for about fifteen minutes. You said two-thirty and it's just two-twenty-seven right now." He took the bags from her.

"Well, whatever. I'm ready." She all but tapped her foot as she waited for him to leave with her.

"Sloan, do you know the Callahans?"

Sloan's eyes narrowed into slits. "No. I don't know them. Perhaps I've heard the name before . . ." She flipped her long, glossy ponytail and made no effort to introduce herself.

The cousins sat on their stools, stunned by her rudeness and her snotty behavior toward Tucker. Tucker seemed to be taking it in stride, though. *But no wonder he was so glad to see us,* thought Hillary. *He's been hanging out with this hag too much!*

"We've just been having a little mini-clinic about sailing here. It seems they have a little sailing project they're planning for this summer. What *is* it that you're doing, exactly, anyway?" he asked, turning back to them.

But before Hillary could say anything, Neeve jumped in.

"Oh, it's this family legacy thing Hillary's cooked up. We're planting a flag . . ."

"It's *nothing*. Nothing at all!" Hillary interrupted rudely. Neeve and the others were taken aback, but Hillary noticed that Sloan had paled beneath her dark tan. The cousins looked at Hillary, confused.

Hillary thought quickly. In desperation, she stood and walked across the room to Sloan and nervously extended her hand. "I'm Hillary. Those are my cousins, Neeve, Kate, and Phoebe Callahan."

Sloan didn't take Hillary's hand, and she finally had to let it drop limply to her side.

"How do you do," Sloan said coldly. "I am Sloan Bicket."

Who says 'How do you do?' anymore? wondered Hillary distractedly. She glanced quickly at the cousins and saw that all of their jaws had dropped. Neeve's face was turning deep red, a rare sighting; Neeve never got embarrassed.

"Well, I guess we're off then," said Tucker, totally clueless as to what had just happened. He came back to the counter, effortlessly carrying Sloan's load of bags in one hand, and laid his money on the counter for the ice cream. "It was fun talking with you guys. Let me know if I can be of any help, anytime!" And then he and Sloan were gone, the bell on the door tinkling quietly behind them as Tucker pulled it gently shut.

There was a moment of stunned silence.

"Oh. My. God." said Phoebe.

"You should have warned me!" cried Neeve.

Hillary returned slowly to her stool. "How could I have?! What could I have said? Neeve, Phoebe, Kate, I'd like to introduce you to our enemy, Sloan Bicket? I didn't even know her first name!"

"But you knew who she *was!*" said Neeve emphatically.

"Yeah, and now she knows our plan, thanks to you!" Hillary spat back.

"Okay, you two. Calm down. Maybe it wasn't that bad. Maybe Sloan didn't catch what Neeve was saying." Kate made soothing gestures with her hands in the air, as if patting down the bad feelings between Neeve and Hillary.

Phoebe snorted. "She sure did. Did you see how she went all white under that self-tanner of hers?"

The girls burst out laughing. "It was fake-and-bake, wasn't it?!" shrieked Neeve. "I thought the same thing the second I saw her!"

Hillary laughed extra-hard, relieved that the tension had been broken. Finally, they quieted down and she sighed.

"Oh well, I guess this'll just make things more interesting. More real," she conceded.

"Oh, it'll be real alright," said Phoebe. "Life jackets. Flares. Spring tides, whatever those are. It'll be *really* real."

Hillary noticed that this time Phoebe didn't say anything about *not* participating in the flag planting. Things were looking good.

CHAPTER SEVEN

It's All Settled

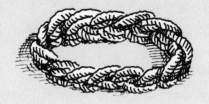

The ride home from town seemed endless and the cool, blue pool beckoned when the girls arrived back at The Sound. They played game after rollicking game of Marco Polo and Shark as the afternoon wound down and the shadows lengthened. Hillary impressed the others with physically daring feats like holding her breath under water for a minute and a half. She was scared to bring up the flag planting; she didn't want to jinx it when things seemed so close to being settled, and no one else brought it up.

Gee had to be at a dinner for her book club, so she sadly left the girls home with Sheila for the night, pressing her perfumed, powdery cheek to each of theirs and leaving a hot-pink kiss mark on each of their foreheads.

For dinner in the kitchen, Sheila served pasta with a thick, red meat sauce on top, salad, and a crunchy loaf of hot, buttery garlic bread. It was all delicious, but the girls held back a little, wanting to save room for their Pig-Out later. "We've got to get some meat on yer bones, all of yas," Sheila rasped, giving a little dry chuckle. "You'll be wastin' away to nothin' with all that swimmin' and bike ridin'."

"Well, we don't want to sink any boats, either, Sheila!" said Neeve lightly.

Sheila's face darkened.

"In sailing clinic, is all I mean. In clinic!" Neeve protested, as the others stared daggers at her.

"Humph!" said Sheila, and she turned back to the stove.

After dinner, Sheila insisted on doing the dishes herself, so the girls decided to gather the Pig-Out supplies and take them down to the bathing pavilion on the end of Gee's dock to watch the boats come in as the light faded. They trotted upstairs and grabbed their jackets and junk food, and wandered back across the yard.

At the pavilion, they sat on the painted wood benches under the peaked roof, and spread the food out on the picnic table: cinnamon donuts, taffy, fudge, some of the leftover green frosting that Kate had made, penny candy, and other assorted junk. Phoebe carefully selected what she wanted, then lined it up neatly in front of her. Hillary just grabbed stuff and made a big pile, while Kate and Neeve simply dipped in and out when they wanted something. The girls chewed and chatted in bliss as they watched the sailors and fishermen return to their home port in town. The sun was low on the pink-streaked horizon, and it was getting chilly, but the girls were comfortable. Little wavelets licked the pilings of the pavilion, and a small plane droned overhead.

"Hey, I have an idea! Stay right here. Don't move, okay?" said Neeve, as she jumped up and began a light run back to the house. Her super-short white surfing shorts looked lavender in the gathering twilight.

"As if I could move!" Kate patted her full stomach.

"Seriously," groaned Phoebe, lying back across the bench. "Just bring me my books and I'll be fine right here for the rest of the summer." She folded her arms neatly behind her head and closed her eyes.

Hillary laughed at them. All of her athletics had given her a pretty good metabolism, so she felt fine after chowing down so many sweets.

When Neeve reappeared she was carrying her new tote bag.

"What's up?" asked Hillary.

"It's the stuff for the ceremony," said Neeve mysteriously.

"Pardon me?" said Phoebe, barely lifting her head.

"The Secret Cousinship Ceremony," replied Neeve, and she began unpacking things from the bag and placing them on the worn wooden table.

"Oh, here we go!" teased Hillary.

Neeve smiled. "Come on, it'll be fun! Have I ever let you down?"

Phoebe's curiosity finally got the better of her and she sat up. They all watched as Neeve took out a green glass candle holder that was covered in netting and had a stubby white candle inside. She plunked it down in the center of the table. Then she distributed a small piece of paper and a pencil to each girl, pulled a worn Cabot's Clam Shack matchbook from her shorts pocket, and put it, too, on the table. Next was a disposable Polaroid camera Kate had bought in town. Finally, Neeve pulled the little Booker's bag out and dumped the four lumpy white rope bracelets onto the table.

Neeve then sat next to Hillary on the bench and lit the ancient candle, which sputtered and flickered before it finally caught. Phoebe and Kate were across from them, and the candle glowed in the middle.

"First of all: photo op. Everyone scrunch together on this bench, c'mon now, don't be shy, and I'll hold the camera, here, like this . . ." The girls did as they were told and Neeve pushed the button. The camera clicked and whirred and the photo slid out of the bottom. Neeve placed it on the table to develop.

"Okay, back to your seats. Here's what we're going to do. Everyone write down a wish for the summer on a piece of paper, then roll it up really well. Don't let anyone else see."

"Hmm, meet a cute boy . . . eat lots of cookies . . . ," said Kate hopefully.

"Shh!" said Neeve as she bent close to the table and crooked her tiny arm around her paper to shield it from view. "Be serious!"

When they had all finished, they looked up at Neeve again.

"Okay, one by one, everyone hold their paper on top of the flame until it gets lit," she instructed. Each girl did as she was told, then held the rapidly burning paper cone in her hand.

"Now, quick! Toss it overboard!" Neeve squealed.

The girls turned, two to a side, and dropped the papers off the dock and into the water, where what remained of the burning paper was extinguished. The scraps floated on the surface for a moment while the girls hung over the railings and watched, then the papers slowly grew sodden and sank.

"Now what?" asked Phoebe, turning back to the table and crossing her legs like a grown-up lady at a tea party.

"Alright, everyone, pick up a bracelet and hold it in your right hand, then cross your arm over, and grab hold of your neighbor's bracelet with your other hand, so we form a circle, 'round like this." Hillary smothered a giggle at the word "neighbor" but did as she was told.

"Where does she get this stuff?" whispered Kate to Hillary, and Hillary smiled.

"Africa?" Hillary suggested jokingly.

"Okay. Now repeat after me. I solemnly swear . . ."

"I solemnly swear . . ."

"To be a good cousin . . ."

"To be a good cousin . . ."

"And to always remember . . ."

"And to always remember . . ."

"That blood is thicker than water . . ."

"That blood is thicker than water . . ."

"And I wholeheartedly promise . . ."

"And I wholeheartedly promise . . ."

"To meet any goal . . ."

"To meet any goal . . ."

At this, Hillary opened one eye to sneak a peek at Phoebe and Kate. Their eyes stayed peacefully closed, which Hillary took as a good sign.

"Set before us . . ."

"Set before us . . ."

"In a grand style . . ."

"In a grand style . . ."

" 'Til death do us part."

" 'Til death do us part."

"We're not getting married, Neeve!" Phoebe blurted.

"I know. That's all; that's the whole thing," said Neeve. "Now each person put on your bracelet and repeat after me . . ."

"Neeve!" pleaded Kate.

But Neeve was absorbed again and didn't look her way. "Cousins forever," she intoned solemnly, as each girl slid her bracelet onto her wrist.

"Cousins forever," the others echoed.

The girls looked around at each other's wrists. Neeve looked pleased, and Kate and Phoebe looked mildly amused.

"So I guess you guys are in for the flag planting, huh?" said Hillary casually, looking around the table, and daring to hope it was true.

"You know it, girl!" said Neeve enthusiastically as she unwrapped a Jolly Rancher.

"Oh, Hillary, I guess so. Do I really have a choice?" whimpered Kate.

Hillary grinned. "Not really."

Phoebe was resigned. "Alright, I'll do it."

"Don't sound *too* excited, Bee!" teased Hillary.

"Don't push your luck, sister! At least I said yes!" snarled Phoebe, but she was smiling.

"Listen you guys, since we're doing it, there's one more thing. I think we should try to do it before our dads come for Pops' birthday." Hillary paused to let this idea sink in. The whole family always came for that one July weekend to celebrate their grandfather's birthday, even though he had died over ten years ago. "It would really be cool if they could see it, planted, y'know?" she added.

Kate sat bolt upright. "But that's less than three weeks from now."

"I know," agreed Hillary. "But I think we can do it."

There was a pause while they absorbed this information.

"Okay," agreed Phoebe finally. "But we have to do it all together. No splitting up," she said. Whether she said this out of fear or some kind of family loyalty, Hillary wasn't sure. But it was a reasonable request.

"Okay."

"Okay, then. To the triumph of the Callahans. Cousins forever!" sang Neeve, and she made a fist and stuck it out in front of her, her white rope bracelet almost glowing in the dusk. Phoebe did the same and placed her fist on top of Neeve's. Then Hillary and Kate. The rope bracelets lined up, looking almost like one long rope, if you squinted, thought Hillary.

"Cousins forever," repeated Kate, Phoebe, and Hillary.

"Hey! Let's quick go see if Gee still has that boat, before it's totally dark," said Hillary impulsively.

"Aye, aye Captain!" agreed Neeve, who was eager to get started on the active part of their quest.

Hillary smiled at the captain reference, and inside, her heart thumped with excitement that the others had agreed to participate in her project. She could already feel the bonds of Callahan-ness growing stronger. *Watch out Bickets!* she thought with glee. *You ain't seen nothing yet!*

The girls left their Pig-Out things as they were, and rose together from the benches.

"She used to keep it in that little shed over there, at the edge of the cove," remembered Phoebe.

"You're right," Hillary agreed. They turned left at the top of the dock and advanced toward the shed in single file, like a small army platoon.

Scraggly bushes and overgrown beach plums made it tough going at the edge of the shore, and it was also a little creepy.

"I wish we had a flashlight," said Kate.

Hillary didn't want the others to get freaked out, so she remained businesslike and purposely misunderstood Kate's comment. "Yeah. Let's make a list of everything we need for our mission. In fact, I think we should stop by the Little Store tomorrow and buy a notebook so we can start keeping track of all the stuff people tell us, and lists of things we need to get or find or do. Kate, maybe you could take charge of the supplies? You're so good at that kind of stuff."

"Oh," said Kate. "Okay." Hillary could tell she was pleased.

"We need to find the flag, for starters," said Neeve as Hillary approached the door of the shed. The shore rocks underfoot were damp with the rising tide, and some were slippery with mossy algae.

"I wonder if it still exists. We might need to make a new one. But how will we know what to make?" wondered Hillary aloud. She was rambling a little, but she wanted to keep Phoebe's and Kate's minds on tangible things instead of on the dark shrubs.

She rattled the rickety wooden door of the shed and it opened with a bang as the warped wood gave way. Sure enough, inside was the little wooden boat. It was nearly impossible to see in the dark — a flashlight *would* have been handy — but Hillary was excited just to know the boat was still there.

"What was that?" cried Kate, jumping. Everyone else jumped, too.

"What?!"

"That sound over there?"

"I don't know!"

In the chaos of the manufactured panic that followed, Hillary was unable to get a good look at the boat. But by the time they'd raced back to the safety of the dock with its tiny flickering candle, hooting and hollering all the way, Hillary had convinced herself that what she'd seen was the finest, most seaworthy vessel as she'd ever clapped eyes on. And that was what she told the others, too.

Not a minute had passed before Sheila came from the other direction, down near the Dorm, and she appeared like a ghost out of the darkness in her pale green cotton shirt.

The girls all jumped, and a new chorus of shrieks erupted, even as they saw it was only Sheila. They were enjoying scaring themselves and were willing to take every opportunity to fan the flames of their fake fear.

"Where were yas? I just came down to check in and tweren't nobody here. It's getting past nine now and I think you ought to come in for the night."

"Oh, we were just . . . over there . . ." Neeve gestured vaguely.

Hillary nodded her head ever-so-slightly in approval. Maybe Neeve was finally learning when to keep her mouth shut.

"Well, ya need to stay away from the water in the dark, now, hear? We can't have ya lost at sea while Herself is out to dinner. Holy mackerel! What would she think?!" Sheila shook her head ruefully, but Hillary sensed she was teasing them just a little.

The girls stood and packed up their things, and followed Sheila up to the house.

As she walked up the hill behind the others, Hillary felt a warm glow of happiness settle over her. For all the cheesiness of Neeve's little bonding ceremony, it had definitely touched something deep inside Hillary, only child that she was. And she was pleased that the girls all had agreed to help her with the flag planting, not to mention that they'd named her their captain. Their quest would be a true test of the Callahan spirit, thought Hillary, and a tribute to their "cousinship," or whatever Neeve wanted to call it.

Among the other scattered remains of the Pig-Out and the ceremony, Hillary found when she got back to her room that she was carrying the Polaroid photo they'd taken. She smiled down at it and neatly tucked it into the frame by her bedside, almost totally obscuring the picture of her with her parents.

Chapter Eight

A Fine Predicament

*H*illary had been wrong. Dead wrong, she corrected herself, as she surveyed Gee's boat in the early morning light. She shook her head in dismay and flicked away a piece of dewy grass that clung to her ankle.

The boat was a disaster. The paint was peeling from the hull outside and the sail was ripped, and inside, its benches were covered in mildew. She couldn't even tell if the boat was actually sailable; she'd need some help dragging it out to do a full inspection. Hillary had woken up so early that she'd had to slip out without disturbing the others. She'd just *had* to have another look at the boat that was to be the means to their success. But now she closed the door slowly and her shoulders sagged in a rare posture of defeat as she trudged back up to the house. Her feet had left tracks in the wet morning grass when she'd walked down the hill, and now she retraced her path, admiring the beauty of the freshly washed morning despite her disappointment. Suddenly, she could hear her father's voice in her head, cheering her on the way he always did at her track meets. "C'mon Hill-Billy! You can do it! You've got what it takes!" *Humph!* thought Hillary. This time she wasn't so sure.

Back in the house, Hillary made a decision as she climbed the stairs to wake the others: She wouldn't let on that the boat was trashed; she'd keep it to herself for now. She just couldn't stand disappointment and worry this early in the morning, and she knew Kate and Phoebe would get themselves in a state about it. She'd find a way to break it to them later.

This postponement turned out to be a good idea after all, because Gee had cleared her schedule and wanted to spend the day with the girls. It would have been misery to try to keep mum around Gee for the day if they all knew about the boat. It was hard enough for Hillary.

Sheila packed a delicious picnic for them, which they divided up among their bike baskets, adding some entertainment gear and heavy wool picnic blankets, too. Then the five of them rode their bikes to the bluff for a few hours of lounging in the sun atop the high and windy cliffs on the ocean side of the island. Hillary and Neeve liked to fly kites and do daredevil stuff at the bluffs, like creep to the edge of the cliff on their stomachs and then hang their heads over and drop rocks down, imagining what it would be like to fall. But Phoebe and Kate spent their time contentedly chatting with Gee, reading and needlepointing in a heathery dip that protected them from the worst of the wind. The morning passed quickly this way, and by the time they'd finished eating and cleaning up, it was well into the afternoon.

On the way home, Gee suggested strawberry picking at Briarpatch Farm, and the girls were game. They claimed their green cardboard boxes from the farmer, and filled them rapidly with the sweet red fruit, then cycled home, careful not to swerve and spill the strawberries.

By three o'clock, Gee had phone calls to return and the girls were on their own once again. Although they were tired, Hillary suggested a ride back to the Little Store to stock up on search supplies, and after much cajoling, she and Neeve were able to get Kate and Phoebe to agree.

Farren was happy to see them and intrigued by the assortment of items that began to accumulate on her counter: sunscreen; a flashlight; a thick, lined school notebook; Scotch tape; flares; binoculars; a cheap weather radio; ChapStick for Phoebe, and, of course, a bit more penny candy.

"What's up?" she finally asked, setting aside the deck of Tarot cards she'd been poring over. "Are you planning a crusade?" Her eyes twinkled in amusement, but she wasn't making fun of them, Hillary noted.

The girls glanced uneasily at each other, unsure of how much to admit. But Neeve couldn't contain herself. "We *are* on a crusade," she burst out. Then she looked at the others and tried to gauge how much she could tell.

"Go for it," Hillary said after a brief pause. And Neeve spilled the whole plan, without mentioning the Bicket name, of course. You could never be sure who was friends with whom on an island.

It was a relief, in a way, to be able to tell an adult everything. And Farren didn't freak out or scold them or anything. She took it all in quietly, asking questions here and there. Then, when they'd finished, she put her chin in her hand and frowned in concentration.

"So you really feel like you need to do this, huh?" she asked finally.

"Yes!" said Hillary eagerly. Neeve nodded for emphasis.

"And how do you think your grandmother would react if she found out?" asked Farren.

"Um . . ." This was the tough spot for Hillary. Judging from Sheila's nervousness, she had to guess Gee would not be pleased. But she had no word on the subject from Gee herself.

"We think it would be better to keep it to ourselves until it's actually done. There's no use worrying her unless it's a fact. That's what I think, anyway," said Neeve. This time it was Hillary who nodded.

"Please don't tell her!" added Kate nervously.

"No, I wouldn't. I always swore I wouldn't grow up to be one of those two-faced adults who acts really cool then rats on kids behind their backs. However, I do think you should tell her your plans. That's my opinion on the subject. Meanwhile, I am here to help you in any way you like." Farren spread her arms wide. "Think of me as the godmother of your crusade. That way I get to live vicariously!"

"What does that mean?" Kate whispered to Phoebe.

"She gets to enjoy our adventures without actually having to do them," Phoebe whispered back.

"Right," said Farren with a wink. The girls were embarrassed she'd overheard them, but quickly recovered. "So what's next?" asked Farren.

"We have to get our boat fixed. It's in pretty bad shape," Hillary admitted with a sigh.

Neeve wheeled around. "What do you mean?" Her eyes were blazing. "I thought you said it was 'shipshape'!"

"I was wrong. It was dark and I got overly excited. I went back again and checked this morning and it's not so great in the daylight." Hillary hung her head. There. It was out in the open.

"So how bad is it?" asked Phoebe. "Because I will not set foot on that contraption unless it's in top condition." She drew herself up imperiously and set her jaw.

"Um, it needs . . . like, a paint job, a lot of cleaning . . . and maybe some leak-proofing. And a new sail." Hillary listed everything she could think of, from what she'd seen this morning.

"Hillary! That's a *lot!*" cried Kate.

"Leak-proofing!" Phoebe muttered, shaking her head.

"So we *are* going to have to get the thing towed somewhere on a trailer, aren't we?" asked Neeve matter-of-factly. She always transitioned quickly from crisis to solution, Hillary noted with admiration.

"I think so," Hillary admitted.

"So Gee's going to have to get involved," continued Neeve.

"Uh-huh," said Hillary. "Unless we find someone who does house calls."

"That could be expensive," warned Phoebe.

"Okay, here's where I come in," interrupted Farren. She reached over to the bulletin board behind the counter and unpinned a small business card. "Go see my friend Smitty, down at the dock in town. He can help you and he's not expensive. He'd probably even do a house call for you. Just tell him I sent you."

Hillary brightened, instantly relieved to have the pressure off. "Thanks!" she said. The others were suddenly pleased, too. Sometimes it did pay to let a grown-up in on a secret. Hillary pocketed the card without glancing at it.

They paid Farren for their supplies and rode home. It was too late to go find this Smitty guy today, but they'd do it in the next day or two.

Back at the house, the girls dumped their stuff in their rooms and ran out for a swim. Then they helped Gee stuff envelopes with invitations for the library benefit, and finally went upstairs to shower and change for dinner. Out on the terrace, Sheila served Hillary's favorite: grilled shrimp fajitas and salad, followed by strawberry shortcake made with the berries they'd picked that day. They all agreed there was nothing better than eating food you've harvested yourself. Then Gee and the girls retired to the sewing room to play Scrabble.

The game really came down to Phoebe, who was, of course, terrific at it, and Gee, who was so obsessed with Scrabble that she'd never let anyone else win — even kids. It was her one ruthless passion in life. Hillary wasn't a big Scrabble fan — being that it was such a quiet and slow sort of game — so she flipped through back issues of *National Geographic* in between turns, while Kate needlepointed and Neeve stood watching CNN and braiding the motionless Phoebe's hair into dozens of tiny braids.

By bedtime, the girls were too tired to sort through their supplies or work on any plans. There was a brief, whispered discussion in Phoebe and Hillary's room about when to go meet Smitty and some excitement about their plan to meet Talbot at Macaroni Beach the next day, and then they parted to get ready for bed.

Moments later, however, Neeve and Kate were alarmed to hear a muffled shriek coming from Hillary and Phoebe's room. They raced back across the hall and found Hillary staring in dismay at something in her hand. It was the card Farren had given them.

"Wha?" Phoebe asked through a mouthful of toothpaste. She'd come in from the bathroom.

Hillary was speechless. She wordlessly handed the card to

Phoebe and then flopped facedown on her bed with a groan. Phoebe's eyes bulged when she read it. She turned into the bathroom and spat into the sink.

"What is it? What?" cried Kate and Neeve.

Phoebe neatly wiped her mouth with a washcloth and then read the card aloud.

"Certified Boat Repairs. All models serviced. Smithson Bicket, proprietor."

CHAPTER NINE

Storms Brewing

"*No!*" Neeve was aghast. "Impossible!"

"Can I see?" asked Kate. Phoebe handed her the card. "Gosh," said Kate. "What do we do?"

Hillary moaned into her bed once more, then sat up with her face propped on her elbows. "Find someone else?" she suggested. She was trying to be like Neeve — upbeat in the face of disaster — but it felt a little weird.

"Someone else who's cheap, makes house calls, and won't need Gee involved? That's a tall order," said Phoebe. She sat on her bed and began removing her mascara with little eye makeup wipes. Phoebe's one vanity was her fairer-than-fair eyelashes; she'd been using mascara since third grade, when a mean boy in her class called her Bald Eye.

"Is it possible that he's not related to the bad Bickets? Maybe it's just a coincidence," offered Kate.

"They're all related. And they're all bad," said Hillary definitively.

Neeve had been silent for a moment while she thought. Finally she spoke up. "You know what I think? I think we should just go for it. Let's just go find him and see what he's like. If he's a jerk or if it seems like a bad idea to get involved with him, we'll bag. But you never know. Maybe it will work out. It's like Pops always said — 'The Lord will provide.'"

"How do you know Pops always said that?" Hillary asked, laughing. "We were only, like, two years old when he died!"

Neeve giggled back. "My dad told me!"

"Neeve's right. Anyway, there's nothing we can do about it now," said Phoebe, glancing at the clock on her bedside table. She gathered up the dirty wipes and went into the bathroom to toss them.

Something about Phoebe's attitude was rubbing Hillary the wrong way. "Do you even care?" she asked when Phoebe came back out of the bathroom. "I mean, it seems like you'd be glad if we couldn't get the boat fixed. Then we wouldn't have to do this whole thing, right?" Hillary's words came out harsher than she'd meant them to, but she suddenly felt kind of mad at Phoebe.

"Hey! Don't take this out on me! It's not my fault he's a Bicket. Anyway, yes, I'd be sort of glad if we couldn't do it, but that's not the point. We're doing it to make *you* happy." Phoebe sat down on her bed and picked up her book, opening it to her marked page and staring down at it as if totally engrossed.

"Well, don't do me any favors!" said Hillary. Now they were really in a fight. She stood up to go into the bathroom.

"Come on, you two. Don't be like this," Kate pleaded.

"I'm not being like anything," said Phoebe, concentrating on her book.

"Hillary . . . ," said Kate. "Please . . ." But Hillary went into the bathroom and closed the door.

"I still say we should go see the guy and see what happens. I'm going to bed," said Neeve, rising from her perch on Hillary's bed. "Make up, you two. No fighting," she called through the bathroom door. She had a very laid-back attitude about cross words; nothing really fazed her. Kate followed, but she wasn't as casual as Neeve. "Yes, please make up," she said fervently, and they left the room.

By the time Hillary emerged from the bathroom, Phoebe had turned out her light. This was when Hillary knew Phoebe and she were really in a fight. Phoebe never went to sleep without reading for at least half an hour. Hillary hadn't meant to take out her disappointment on Phoebe, and now she felt bad.

"Bee?" she whispered in the dark. But there was no reply.

By lunchtime the next day, Hillary and Phoebe had reached an uneasy truce. The night's sleep had done them some good, and Hillary had made a big effort to be nice to Phoebe all morning. She didn't even wake her up when she got up. She just tiptoed quietly out of the room and drew the door closed behind her so Phoebe could sleep on, undisturbed.

After Phoebe awoke around ten, Neeve's teasing and Kate's peacemaking aided in Hillary's apology efforts, and Hillary had generously helped Phoebe remove all the braids Neeve had done in her hair. Hillary complimented Phoebe's new 'do, and by the time the girls had gotten on their bikes to go meet Talbot at the beach, Phoebe had apologized to Hillary, too, and they were on pretty good terms again.

But Hillary had not enjoyed the short-lived conflict, and it made her see how quickly a fight could escalate and get out of control when people were living in such close proximity to one another. It gave her some sympathy for her parents and even a weird kind of understanding of the Bicket/Callahan divide.

After about a mile and a half of riding along Fisher's Path toward town, the girls turned left onto the narrow Huckleberry Lane to ride across Gull to the island's only real ocean beach. The strange shape of the island, and its direct exposure to the battering waves of the Atlantic, had left Gull with cliffs all along its eastern shore, save for a small section where the island's "wings" converged and created a little protected area. Here, the Atlantic had dumped sand over the years. The resulting beach, known as Macaroni Beach, was the only place you could really go for ocean swimming and lying on a wide expanse of sand. Consequently, it could get very crowded on certain summer days. But for now, on a weekday in mid-June, things at Macaroni would be quiet.

Hardly any cars were on the road, so the girls sat up and

rode no hands, crisscrossing in big, loopy S-shapes along the empty country road. There were few houses on this part of the island because the coastline was part of the National Seashore preserve that prohibited houses from being built along the ocean. The only structures were old farms — and houses and barns were not allowed to be rebuilt if they came down.

The girls passed a farmer on his tractor who was fertilizing his rows of baby potato plants; he waved and the girls waved back. Every now and then, at the end of a driveway or dirt road, they'd see a wooden cart full of early summer produce for sale — strawberries, wildflowers in bunches, some baby carrots, honey.

The road began to rise as the girls approached the beach, and they all had to stand on their pedals to coax the ancient bikes up the small hill and into the parking lot. To the right was a bike rack and past it, The Snack: a small wooden shack that served grilled, fried, and frozen foods every day of the summer between twelve and four. The enticing aroma of cooking french fries drifted toward them on the breeze, mingling with the smell of the blooming honeysuckle bushes that clustered and climbed rambunctiously around the fences at the edges of the nearly empty parking lot. They reached the top of the hill and the beach spread out before them, anchored by the tall white lifeguard stand in the middle, and dotted here and there with a few small clumps of people sunning, chatting, reading, and sleeping. Beyond the small breakers, the navy blue ocean was flat but ruffled in the breeze.

The noon whistle wailed off in the distance, and Hillary

glanced at her watch. Was it already twelve? But no, it was just a quarter to. Maybe the firemen were hungry so they set it off a little early today, she thought absently.

Talbot was sitting with a group of kids at one of the picnic benches, and he waved vigorously at the Callahans when he saw them arrive. The girls parked their bikes and strolled over, and he made introductions all around. His friends were very nice and outgoing — Neeve in particular was excited to meet some new people — but Talbot and the cousins quickly moved to their own table so they could discuss their flag project.

This time, Hillary had the honor of explaining their quest; as Neeve had done before her, she did not reveal the Bicket name in describing it. For all she knew, Sloan could be Talbot's best friend. But she did let on that their rival now knew about the project and that this worried the cousins. She also described the state of their boat and asked him what he thought they should do about it.

Talbot knew Smitty, too, because he'd sold Talbot's dad his boat. "He's chill," he said, nodding. "I bet he'd help you without getting any adults involved. You should go check him out."

"Yeah . . ." Hillary was distracted by Smitty's Bicket connection but she couldn't mention it.

"So do you guys know where you're going?" asked Talbot.

"Sort of," said Neeve. "We can't remember the name of it, but it's the same shape as Gull. That's all we know."

"Hmm. One of the tidal islands off North Wing, toward town, is kinda Gull-shaped. You're gonna have to look it up on a chart, though. Do you have one? 'Cause my dad has lots," offered Talbot.

"Actually, they have them at the library, so we thought we'd just go there," said Phoebe.

"Okay. Just remember, if it's a tidal island, you're going to have to time it right, when you go. Tidal islands change shape — or even disappear under water — when the tide is in. Especially when the spring tide is running. But the charts should be able to tell you all this."

Phoebe had commandeered their new notebook and designated herself Chief Research Officer, so she was jotting down notes on a page headed TALBOT. Hillary looked over her shoulder approvingly, glad that she was getting it all down, and even gladder that she was showing so much interest. Of course, this note-taking and research was the part of the quest that appealed to Phoebe the most. Hillary dreaded the day they'd actually have to get Phoebe (not to mention Kate) into a boat to go plant the flag. She sighed aloud.

"What?" asked Neeve, hearing Hillary's sigh.

"Oh, I was just thinking, that's all," Hillary replied. She didn't want to get them on the safety issue or they'd never get off it, so she asked another question. "Talbot, if we got some copies of the, um, charts and showed them to you, would you be able to help us figure out our course and stuff?"

"Yeah, mon. No problem." Hillary and Neeve shared a smile at Talbot's lapse into Jamaica-speak. Then he slapped his forehead. "Duh! I just thought of something. You've got to look at some old charts from when your dads were still doing this, so you can compare . . ."

Suddenly a shadow fell across their table. The girls looked up. It was Sloan Bicket.

"Hello, Talbot," she said formally.

"Hey, Sloan," said Talbot wearily. Hillary quickly stifled an involuntary smile. Talbot wasn't best buds with Sloan, that much was clear from the lack of enthusiasm in his greeting.

Sloan narrowed her eyes and looked around the table at the Callahans. "Hanging out with the tourists today, are we, Talbot? You're like the one-man Gull Island welcoming committee." She folded her arms across her chest, as if challenging Talbot to correct her.

Talbot didn't take the bait. "Have you met the Callahan cousins? Guys, this is Sloan Bicket." Talbot waved his hand at her in a disinterested way. "The unofficial queen of Gull Island," he added.

Sloan sneered at him. "Whatever that's supposed to mean. But yeah, we know each other. Our families go *way back*. Unlike some people's." She stared pointedly at Talbot.

Talbot shrugged. "At least I haven't spent my life trapped in one place."

Sloan fumed in silence, then looked directly at Neeve. "So the contest is on again?" she said.

Neeve was momentarily speechless. She looked at Hillary for a split second for guidance, and then drew herself up to her full height (which wasn't substantial, especially considering that she was seated). "Yes. May the best family win," she said, looking Sloan in the eye.

Hillary glanced at Talbot and saw understanding dawn on his face. Now he knew who the Callahans were competing against. He winked at Hillary and she grinned back.

"Yes. Well, there's really no contest. After all, the Callahans are just a summer family. And no matter how many summers you've spent here, you're not true Islanders 'til you've lived here year-round for generations." Sloan smirked in satisfaction. And before Neeve could reply, Sloan turned to Talbot again. "I'm surprised to see you sitting here entertaining tourists when Booker's is burning to the ground downtown," she announced calmly, as if relishing the news.

"What?!" Talbot jumped to his feet. "What are you talking about?"

"Just what I said," said Sloan. "I just came from town and Booker's is surrounded by fire engines, engulfed in flames."

"I gotta go!" cried Talbot. "Sorry guys! I'll check ya later!" He raced down the walkway to the bike rack, grabbed his mountain bike, and tore off down the hill.

Sloan spun on her heel, mission accomplished, and went to place her order at The Snack's counter without so much as another word to the Callahans.

The girls looked at each other in shock.

"Come to think of it, I did hear the fire whistle blow just when we got here," said Hillary with a frown.

"Fire? *Contest?*" whispered Kate urgently. "I don't know

which is worse!" She stole a glance at Sloan's back, up at the counter.

"I thought the tourist part was the worst, myself," said Neeve. "That was just nasty! I mean, *as if!* Our family's been here just as long as hers; maybe even longer! And, what, you have to suffer through dozens of boring, cold winters here just to earn the right to call yourself an islander? That's baloney!"

"Look, it's not about how much time you spend on Gull. It's what you do with your time and how you behave while you're here," said Hillary in a low voice. The others leaned in to hear her. "The Callahans are classier than the Bickets and we know it. People *like* us. And most people *don't* like the Bickets. Just look at how rude Sloan is. Could you *ever* imagine talking to people the way she does?" Hillary looked around the table and all the girls solemnly shook their heads.

Neeve sat back and cracked a small smile. "You sound just like Gee."

Hillary was pleased at the comparison. She grinned and continued. "In a way it's good that we now know *for sure* that Sloan's got her own flag-planting plans. We know what we're up against."

"Look, it's a total bummer if there's a fire, but there's nothing we can do about it," said Neeve rationally. "As for *Sloan*," Neeve drawled her name in an imitation of Sloan's snotty voice, "I say *bring it on,* girl! We'll definitely win. Now let's wait 'til she's done up there and then we'll order some lunch and hang on the beach for a while. We can call Talbot when we get home to make sure everything's okay."

"Aren't you guys scared, now that Sloan's doing it too?" asked Kate with a worried expression on her face. She looked at each of the others to see how they felt.

"Surprisingly, no," said Phoebe quietly, her jaw set. "If there's one thing that's making me want to do this flag thing, it's her. The more I see of her the more I want to get her."

"Same," agreed Hillary.

"Oh dear," whimpered Kate.

"But listen, you guys, we've got to get on this, and fast! Now that Sloan's in the running, we need to be organized and ready to go soon! We have to get our flag planted first. Then, if she ever does actually make it out there, she'll see we were already there." Sloan had fanned the flames of Hillary's natural competitiveness, and now Hillary was raring to go.

"But what do we do if she takes our flag out and plants hers?" asked Kate.

"We just make darn sure that it's our flag that's planted when our dads get here!" said Hillary. "And we keep checking, for the rest of the summer!"

"Yeah!" agreed Neeve. "So what next?"

"We've got to find the flag," said Hillary. She was guessing that if they had the actual *thing* that they needed to plant, it would spur them on to get the other details finalized. She hoped she was right.

CHAPTER TEN
The Irish

$\mathcal{A}$fter lunch at The Snack and an hour of body-surfing (Neeve and Hillary) and wading in the tide pools (Phoebe and Kate), the girls rode back to The Sound. Their afternoon task was to search the attics and the garage for the Callahan family flag. With Sloan in the running there was no more time to dilly-dally.

The free-standing, barnlike garage had slots for three cars, and stuff hanging all over its walls — buoys, life jackets, ancient bicycle pumps, gardening tools, rickety beach chairs, coiled hoses, and other accumulated junk. However, Mr. Addison, the part-time gardener, kept it very orderly, so the girls quickly saw that there was no flag to be found there. Hillary bravely scaled a wooden ladder to peer around the rafters up by the roof, where old sleds and shutters and other flat stuff were stored, but she didn't find anything there, either.

The girls exited, not too disappointed yet, and made their way into the house. In the kitchen, Neeve placed a quick call to Booker's to make sure it was still standing. It turned out that Sloan had actually been right — there had been some smoke and two fire engines — but it had only been a small fire in a trash can in the basement, and it had been quickly extinguished. No one was hurt and nothing was harmed, thanks to a quick-thinking sales clerk. Relieved, the girls climbed quickly up to the third floor to search the attics.

Each end of the third floor had a long, peak-roofed attic; in between them were three tiny bathrooms and six little bedrooms. Sheila lived in some of these rooms, but luckily, she wasn't home, so the girls didn't have to make up a reason for being up there.

They entered the attic wing above Gee's suite first, and fanned out to begin peeking into trunks and boxes. The attic was crammed full of old toys and furniture, boxes of outdated clothes and books, and lots of sundry bits and pieces that had migrated up there after the girls' dads and aunts and uncles had grown up.

"What a mess," said Phoebe, wrinkling her nose in distaste. But she grudgingly warmed to the search when she discovered a trove of antique leather-bound books.

"Hey, look at this cute pillow!" Kate called out at one point. She'd been up once already this summer, so she knew where to look for things that interested her.

"I wonder who went to all these places?" Neeve was impressed, studying a steamer trunk stickered with all kinds of foreign decals.

"Focus!" Hillary called back. "We're looking for the flag, not junk!"

It was stuffy up there, though, and hot, and the girls' enthusiasm for the project quickly waned.

After twenty minutes, Neeve sat down heavily on the steamer trunk and blew air up from her lower lip to cool her perspiring forehead. Her black bangs barely fluttered, pasted as they were to her forehead. "I hate to say it, but I think we should bag."

Hillary stood for a moment with her hands on her hips, as if calculating whether or not to press onward. She was disappointed to stop searching, but she was also starting to get claustrophobia. Had it been Phoebe or Kate who had suggested they bag, Hillary would have insisted they forge onward. But since it was Neeve, Hillary, too, caved.

"I guess you're right," she said, surveying the packed room. "Even if it is here, we'll never find it."

Phoebe fanned her face with an old copy of *Life* magazine. "We'd melt first."

Kate was making a bundle of things she wanted to take downstairs. "Let's go for a swim, instead. We can grab some towels on the way down."

Back on the second floor, Hillary volunteered to get the towels. As she trudged slowly back down the corridor from the linen closet to her room to change, she looked at the photographs along the wall. In her mind, she was already apologizing to the previous generations of Callahans for failing to uphold their name. Suddenly, she stopped in her tracks and the towels spilled from her arms to the floor.

She reached to lift one of the photos off the wall, and stumbled over the towels to flick on the overhead light.

"Hey, you guys . . . ," she called, clutching the photo in her hand. "Guys!"

The others came wandering back out of their rooms. "What?" asked Neeve.

"Look at this," Hillary commanded, handing over the photo to her. Phoebe and Kate leaned in next to her and they all peered at the picture. It was their dads, all in their mid-teens, more or less. They were wearing bathing suits and standing proudly on a beach on an island out in the sound. Neeve's father was clutching a pole that was stuck in the ground at a jaunty angle, topped by a flag that was flying just outside the frame of the picture.

"No. Way," said Neeve seriously.

"Is that the flag?" whispered Kate. "Who do you think took this?"

"Uncle Lou. That's why he's not in the photo."

Hillary studied the picture. "It's too bad you can't see what's *on* the flag."

"Actually, I don't think it matters," said Phoebe. "At least we know how tall it was, and approximately how big the flag was." She glanced over Hillary's shoulder at the photo again. "It looks like they used a broom handle for the pole, and . . ."

Kate chimed in, "Sail cloth for the flag part! We can do that! It'll be easy!"

"But what do we do for a design?" asked Hillary, warming to the idea.

They were all silent for a moment while they thought. Then Phoebe spoke up. "How about if we paint CALLAHAN in block letters, like on the sign at the bottom of the driveway? And then we can look up our family crest in one of those Irish history books Gee has in her library and put that on, too. Kate, you could paint that for us, right?"

Everyone agreed. "And a family motto," added Hillary. *So what if it's not the original flag!* she decided. *We can make a really cool one that will blow those Bickets away!*

With their swim postponed indefinitely, the girls galloped downstairs to the library. Phoebe walked knowledgeably right to the section of Gee's shelves that held the Irish books, and she withdrew the huge stack and doled them out to everyone.

The girls settled themselves in the deep, squishy couches and club chairs around the room and began to pore over the books, looking for information about the origins of their family name.

Neeve was looking at a book of fairy tales, her own elfish looks accentuated by the way she'd curled into a tiny ball in one corner of a couch. Now and then she'd pipe up with a snippet of legend, but none of it had to do with the Callahans.

Hillary and Kate were looking at big, glossy photographic books of Ireland, and while Hillary was entranced by the images of the rugged countryside of the West Coast, Kate would sigh aloud at depictions of stained glass windows in churches or beautiful hand-knit Irish sweaters. Every now and then, Hillary would stare longingly at the rambling row of family photo albums on Gee's book shelf. She was dying to spend a while, poring over them and searching for photos of her dad and herself, reaffirming their places in the family. But Phoebe was a tough taskmaster, and Hillary's photo album perusal would not be considered valid research for the cause, so she'd resist the urge.

Of course, Phoebe was all business. After about ten minutes of poring over a dense book of Irish history, she shouted, "Aha!"

The others clambered out of their seats and gathered around her. "What?" they asked.

"I found something. Here . . . let me just . . . Okay. The Callahans were from Munster, Ireland, originally. King Callahan was King of Munster — I think that's the Southwest of the country . . ." Phoebe flipped to an old map at the beginning of her book for reference. "Yeah. And this was in the 900s AD. Um . . . lots of battles . . . Oh, cool. The name comes from the Irish word for strife."

"I don't think that's cool," said Kate.

"Well, whatever. The ancient Callahans had a lifelong battle with the MacCarthy clan . . ."

"Kind of like us with the Bickets!" said Neeve.

Phoebe nodded, and continued. "Let's see . . . castles . . . mansions . . . cattle raids . . . it's kind of interesting but there's nothing about the family motto or crest. We're going to have to go to the library."

"What are yas up to?" Sheila had appeared in the doorway without their noticing, and they all jumped when they heard her. Her arms were filled with the towels Hillary had dropped on the floor upstairs.

"Hi, Sheila. We're just, um . . ." Neeve was at a loss for words for possibly the first time in her life.

"Just doing some research," said Phoebe innocently.

Sheila crossed the room to peer at their books. "Oh, learnin' about the old country, are yas? I could tell you a thing or two, I'm sure." She grinned. "What do ya have there?" she asked Kate, whose finger was still marking the page in her book.

Kate opened her book to a page of Irish sweater designs.

"Ah, the Aran jumper," said Sheila with a twinkle in her eye. "Do yas know all about those?"

Neeve had recovered her gift of gab. "Yes. There are family patterns, or something, right?"

Sheila smiled. "True. The Aran jumpers, what you call 'Irish sweaters' over here, they were originally knit by fishermen's wives in distinct family patterns. The men would wear them out on the boats because they kept them warm and the lanolin in the lambs' wool made the sea water and rain bead off. But the real thing was the patterns. If someone was lost at sea or fell overboard and sank, and the body turned up later all decomposed, ya could always tell who it was by the pattern in the sweater."

"Gross!" cried Kate in alarm.

"If memory serves me, I think the Callahan family pattern has a honeycomb — representin' work — and some zigzags — representin' the ups and downs of married life." Sheila cackled and stood up. "Not that I'd know much about that, t'anks be to God! Now are yas wantin' these towels, or should I replace 'em?"

"Uh, we'll keep them. Thanks, Sheila. Sorry about just dropping them up there," said Hillary apologetically.

But Phoebe was still thinking about all of their new information. "Sheila, why are all the Irish stories so bloody and deadly? All this fighting and stuff?"

Sheila paused thoughtfully for a moment. "I guess because we're loyal and stubborn and independent, as a race. And we have long memories. We're not a people to forget past wrongs."

The girls exchanged a knowing look, but Sheila intercepted it. "Now don't yas be thinkin' that's alright, neither. The Irish can be pigheaded and stupid about grudges, and they've wasted a lot of energy and talk over the years just beatin' stories to death. Use yer heads. Don't be that way. Now I'm off to make the supper." And she turned on her heel and departed as abruptly as she'd arrived.

The girls breathed a sigh of relief after she'd left.

"I've got to get outside," said Hillary. "I don't even care if we swim or jump on the tramp or go for a bike ride. I just need to be outdoors for a while. But listen, you guys. We've got to go see Smitty. We've got to keep the momentum going. There's no time to waste."

"We'll go tomorrow," said Neeve.

Everyone agreed, and they quickly stowed their books back on the shelf and wandered outside in the late afternoon sunlight, eager to forget about family grudges and bad Irish traits for a while.

CHAPTER ELEVEN

Smitty

Friday was overcast and cool, and after much debate, the girls reluctantly decided the weather wasn't good enough to risk riding into town in search of Smitty. So they took a day off from their quest. Gee, oblivious to their struggles, took them to lunch in town and to the movies, where popcorn, Twizzlers, and a love story did much to distract them.

On Saturday, however, the day was gorgeous and sparkling — with all the clouds washed out to sea. And there was no excuse for them not to ride their bikes to town in search of Smitty.

But Hillary had a knot in her stomach. She was nervous about approaching the man, nervous that he wouldn't help them and nervous that he would. She was furious at herself for what she felt was cowardice, but she couldn't help it. However, she forced a brave face, because that was what the others needed and expected, and she led the way to the docks in town.

When they located Smitty's headquarters — a one-room shack on the south dock just past the ferry slip — the girls paused. It had a rundown appearance, with boat parts left messily about, and rotting shingles on its siding, and a kind of abandoned look. But issuing from inside was a rich baritone voice singing opera, a sophisticated and lovely sound that contrasted mightily with the business's appearance.

The girls looked at one another, and Hillary drew a deep breath. Even Neeve didn't seem to be willing to take the lead on this one. Hillary stepped up to the door and knocked, clearly wishing that there would be no answer.

But the singing stopped and a voice bellowed from inside. "Enter! Yonder portal is ajar!"

The girls giggled, and Hillary pushed the door open.

Inside, buoys hung from the low rafters and shelves were stuffed full of boxes overflowing with boat supplies and parts. There was a pot-bellied stove in the near corner that was unlit, and an ancient hooked rug on the floor that depicted some fuzzy-looking schooner. A high wooden counter, much scratched and abused, hid a work area from view. As the girls entered, a short, bald, extremely rotund man stood up from the workbench and peered over the counter at them with a huge grin on his face. Although he was missing a number of teeth and his skin seemed permanently sunburned into dark leather, he had a jolly look to him and the girls were instantly entranced.

"Ah, now, are you the garden club ladies come to do my window boxes?" he said in his deep voice, but there was a mischievous twinkle in his eye and they knew he was joking.

"No . . . ," laughed Hillary.

"Publishers Clearing House Sweepstakes? I'm your big winner?!" He cried in jest. "Oh, praise the Lord! My ship has come in!" He started to dance a little jig in the cramped area behind the counter.

The girls laughed harder. "No . . . we're just . . ."

The man put his hands on his hips and pretended to glare at them. "You mean I've lost again?" he cried. "How can you be so cruel as to deliver the news in person? Are you hoping I'll weep right in front of you?" He was encouraged by how much he was cracking them up, but when he took a breath to begin again, Neeve jumped in.

"We need your help!" she shouted with a smile.

"Well. Why didn't you say so instead of starting in with all this lottery jazz?" He folded his small, pudgy hands on the counter and smiled calmly. "Smithson Bicket, at your service. What can I do for you ladies today?"

They were taken aback once again when reminded of his name. His friendliness, such a contrast to Sloan's ice queen demeanor, had made them momentarily forget who he was.

"Farren sent us . . . ," offered Neeve.

"We have a boat that's in need of repair . . . ," began Hillary.

"In *great* need . . . ," added Phoebe.

"And we were wondering if you could help us?" finished Hillary.

"I would like nothing more," he beamed. "Any friend of Farren's is a friend of mine. What kind of a craft is it, now?"

"Well, I don't know, actually. It's a really small, old wooden sailboat. It's our grandmother's and she's had it forever."

"Now who would that be, your grandmother? I know everyone on the island," Smitty asked in a friendly manner. He clasped his hands across his ball-shaped tummy and peacefully awaited their answer.

The girls glanced uneasily at each other. They hadn't thought the truth would have to come out so soon.

"Uh . . . Mrs. Callahan. Samantha Callahan," offered Hillary tentatively. She practically hunched her shoulders in self-protection, expecting to be kicked out of the shop then and there. But that was not to be the case.

"Mrs. Callahan's your grandmother!" cried Smitty. "You lucky little sprogs! Was there ever a greater woman on this island? This calls for a celebration!" He gathered an old pipe and a pouch of tobacco from his workbench and hustled them all outdoors so he could have a smoke.

Out in the bright morning sunlight, the girls were giddy with relief. Pipe in hand, Smitty regaled them with tales of their grandmother's legendary generosity and the Callahan family's role in various successful island projects.

The girls exchanged nervous glances until Hillary finally screwed up her courage and asked the question that was on all of their minds. "Um . . . Mr. . . . Smitty? Aren't you a Bicket? I mean, how come you and our grandmother are friends? Because, we've always heard there's . . ."

But Smitty interrupted her with an impatient wave of his pipe. "Rubbish. That's all. Water under the bridge. My cousin Robert's got a chip on his shoulder and a memory like an elephant. I must say, I wouldn't even speak to him if he weren't my biggest customer, what with my servicing the delivery boats for the store and all. But he pays the rent, as it were, so I can't look that gift-horse in the mouth. Anyhoo, why don't we get down to brass tacks, then, shall we? Tell me more about this little ship of yours."

Hillary was dubious about Smitty's take on Bicket/Callahan relations, but she let it go. She didn't want to make too much of it since they needed his help. She explained the boat's condition, and Smitty asked a few questions to ascertain the extent of the problems. He didn't think it sounded as dire as Hillary did; in fact, he said, they could get started on it themselves, with a few supplies from him and a few things from the hardware store. Phoebe whipped out the notebook and made a list of the items they'd need. Sandpaper, caulk, putty knives, boat paint, a new sail, she wrote in a neat column. Then she made a list of instructions, scribbling quickly now to keep up with Smitty's long-winded advice. He was just volunteering to make a house call after all when they were interrupted by the *beep, beep, beep*ing of a truck in reverse.

Everyone turned to look, and it was a dark green Suburban

with a trailer, towing a sleek little wooden motorboat, backing onto the dock. When it reached Smitty's ramp, where boats could be lowered onto his work dock, it stopped. The passenger door was flung open and a long, tan leg extended down, down, until . . . Sloan appeared out of the truck.

"Here we go again," muttered Neeve. The others' eyes widened in dread.

Smitty, on seeing Sloan, became very flustered. He scampered across to her, surprisingly light on his feet for all his girth, and began chattering at her in a high, nervous voice. He glanced awkwardly over his shoulder at the Callahans, as if he wished they wouldn't still be there when he turned, but of course they were.

"Smithson, I need this boat repaired immediately," Sloan drawled in her bored yet commanding voice. Her eyes flicked across the girls in acknowledgment of their presence, but she didn't say hello, as usual. "I have a very important project, a family project, that I need it for and I can't be delayed."

The girls exchanged glances.

"Of course, Sloan, of course, anything I can do for you. You know I'm at your service," Smitty whined in an eager-to-please voice.

Then the driver's side door of the Suburban opened and Tucker emerged. He smiled awkwardly at the Callahans, and Hillary, on seeing him, drew a sharp breath. "Oh!" she said. "Hi." Hillary was distracted because she wanted to continue to eavesdrop on Sloan's conversation with Smitty. She wanted to know what Sloan's timetable was for planting the flag.

But Tucker was crossing the dock to greet the girls, friendly as ever. "I'm sorry we haven't seen more of each other," he said to the cousins. "I'm always getting roped into one duty or another over at the Bickets'." He rolled his eyes toward Sloan.

Hillary smiled in understanding. "That's okay. Are you doing alright over there?" She spoke quietly so Sloan wouldn't hear her.

"Yeah, it's fine. The garage apartment is really nice and I actually do get some time to myself, here and there, to go out on the water. I've gotten to know my way around the sound pretty well now." Tucker seemed fine, to Hillary's relief.

"So what's all this about?" asked Neeve, jutting her chin toward Sloan.

"Ah, some little project or other. Sloan always has something up her sleeve, but I never really get the full story." Tucker shaded his eyes in the midday sun and looked back over at Sloan and Smitty, still deep in conversation. He looked back at the Callahans and smiled widely. "I'm just here to do the heavy lifting."

The girls smiled back, feeling a little sorry for him. "Hey, you should come for dinner at our house one night!" said Neeve spontaneously.

"Yeah!" the others chimed in.

Tucker was truly pleased, they could tell. "Thanks. That would be really nice," he said. "Maybe one night next week?"

"Whenever! We'll just pick a night when we see you at clinic on Monday," said Neeve.

It had gotten hot standing on the dock in the blaring sun,

and Phoebe was feeling spent, indoor creature that she was. "Let's go, you guys," she suggested.

"Yeah, I'll just go ask Smitty for those things we need and see if we can set a date for his house call," Hillary volunteered. She knew no one else would be willing to approach him while he was talking with Sloan, so she figured it might as well be her.

She crossed the dock to the trailer just in time to hear Sloan saying rudely, "I've got to get to that island as soon as possible, Smithson. My father said I should tell you not to forget or pull any of your lazy tricks. He said he knows how you can be — all talk and no action. This boat's got to be ready on time!" Hillary stood to the side, waiting politely for a break in their conversation. Lazy tricks? All talk? *Uh-oh,* thought Hillary.

"Of course not, Sloan. I mean, of course it will be ready," Smitty was saying.

"Good. Now where shall I have Tucker put it?" Sloan asked.

Finally Hillary could wait no more. "Excuse me, Smitty?" she interjected.

Smitty jumped. He had completely forgotten the Callahans were still there. "Yes, may I help you?" Smitty was acting like he'd never seen Hillary before. *Yikes! Maybe Sloan has a point about his memory,* thought Hillary.

"Just those things you said we needed, please, so we can be on our way? And also, we need to book your house call?"

Sloan had been taking in the whole conversation. Suddenly it seemed she could no longer contain herself. "I'm surprised a bunch of tourists would ever find a place like this. I'm also shocked that you have the nerve to come here and ask for help from someone who is clearly *not* on your team," Sloan hissed.

Hillary was speechless for a moment. "It's a free country!" she finally said, lamely.

Smitty looked nervously at Sloan and then back at Hillary. "Right this way, miss . . . uh . . . young lady." He clearly didn't want to announce the name "Callahan" right in front of Sloan; he had no way of knowing that Sloan already knew it. Smitty nearly dragged Hillary into the shop in his rush to get rid of her.

Inside the store, it took a moment for Hillary's eyes to re-adjust to the dimness. Her knees shivered from the encounter with Sloan. Oh, how she wished she could've thought of a better comeback. That one was so second grade!

Meanwhile, Smitty was distracted. He scurried around, loading supplies into a cardboard box. "I'll just put it on Mrs. Callahan's account, then," he said quickly, eager to finish the transaction. He thrust the box into Hillary's arms.

"Um . . ." Hillary wasn't sure. "Okay . . . And about our meeting?"

"Right," he said briskly. "Call me at the beginning of next week and we'll set a time. I've got oodles of things to do, so we'll have to squeeze you in somewhere." He spun on his heel and whisked out the door.

Gosh, those Bickets must be good customers, thought Hillary, shaking her head. *They've got some power over poor Smitty.*

Back outside, Smitty, Tucker, and Sloan were now engrossed

in unloading Sloan's boat, so the girls took off without saying goodbye. As they walked their bikes up Market Street, Hillary filled in the others on her exchange with Sloan.

"Hey, I think I already know the answer to this question, but . . . if it sounds like Sloan knows where the island is, maybe we should just ask her . . . ?" suggested Kate.

The other three turned on her. "Are you nuts?!" shouted Neeve.

Kate laughed and put her hands up in the air to surrender. "Okay, okay, just checking. But here's another thing: What do we do with Sloan's actual flag if she plants hers first?" asked Kate. "I mean, once we pull it out and plant ours."

"Well . . . I know that at one point our dads used to do funny stuff with the Bickets' flag. Like I think Neeve's dad planted it in the graveyard one time," offered Hillary.

"Ooh, we are definitely *not* doing that!" declared Kate with a shiver.

"And I think one time, Phoebe, *your* dad dipped the Bickets' flag in sugar water to try to get bees to swarm over it."

Everyone laughed. "Brilliant! I wonder if it worked!" shrieked Neeve.

"But towards the end, they would just turn the other person's flag upside down or something. Like bury the flag part in the sand." Hillary had listened eagerly to every detail her dad had told her about this game over the years. His childhood stories about Gull and all of his brothers and sisters had filled her mind with the imagined joys of spending summers in a sprawling house with a sprawling family, so unlike her own quiet family cottage back home.

"That's what we should do, if she beats us there," said Phoebe sensibly. "Just jam it in the ground. It's the easiest, and also the most symbolic."

"Eat dirt, Bickets!" yelled Neeve impulsively, then she clapped her hand over her mouth and looked around the town to see if anyone had heard her. When it was clear that no one had, all the girls laughed so hard they got cramps in their sides.

Over at the hardware store, they picked up some really nice green paint for the boat, and a few smaller cans of other colors for extra decoration. They decided to wait on buying a sail; they'd bring in the remains of the old one next week so they could match it, since they had no idea what size to get or anything. Then they cycled home for sandwiches by the pool and a long, cool swim.

Later, Gee took them to the early evening mass at the Cliff Church, and then to Cabot's for dinner afterward, which was a Callahan family Saturday night tradition. Gee had invited Father Ryan to join them when they'd seen him outside the church after mass, and it turned out to be really fun that he'd come along. He regaled them with great Gull stories, and the girls were particularly enraptured by his descriptions of the blessing of the fleet — an annual Gull Island tradition in which all the religious clergy on the island gathered at the dock on Memorial Day and blessed all the boats that came to the harbor. Hillary could tell that Phoebe and Kate thought it would be a good idea to ask Father Ryan to bless their boat, but they kept mum on the subject, so as not to alert Gee to their flag-planting project.

Over dessert, Father Ryan asked the girls what their plans were for keeping busy during their stay on Gull.

Hillary purposely did not look at the others. They could hardly tell him about the flag-planting. "Um . . . ," she began awkwardly.

"Well, we start sailing clinic on Monday, which should be fun," said Neeve enthusiastically.

Quick thinking, Neeve, thought Hillary. She flashed her a smile.

"Oh, that's wonderful!" said Father Ryan. "Sailing is a skill that will last you a lifetime. Now, let's see, I know there are some other children in the parish who are doing that, too, this summer. Hmm . . ." He was thoughtful for a moment and everyone waited politely. The girls didn't expect to know who he was thinking of, but they each assumed Gee would make sure they sought out whoever it was that he mentioned.

"Aha!" he said finally. "The Bickets' girl. Sloan! She'll be at clinic this summer." He smiled at them, proud of his memory. No one said anything, but before things could get awkward, Gee signaled the waitress for the check and waved at an acquaintance across the restaurant.

"Look, Father, there's Mrs. Coffin. Let's go say hello when

we finish. I'd like to talk to her about the White Elephant sale we're having at the church in August."

Hillary breathed a sigh of relief that Gee had changed the subject. She couldn't bear having to make empty promises to Father Ryan about befriending Sloan. She glanced at the others and they all shared a small smile, sure that they each felt the same way.

By bedtime that night, a collective dread had settled over the foursome. Would Sloan now be a part of their daily activities?

CHAPTER TWELVE

Getting Their Bearings

$\mathcal{M}$onday, the first day of clinic, dawned foggy and chilly. Neeve's alarm went off at seven o'clock, and all the girls rose sluggishly, one by one, to get dressed. Neeve, of course, managed to bring international flair to her sailing outfit — donning a tie-dyed Chinese tank top over a long-sleeved purple leotard and cut-off red Sweetie Sweats for shorts. Kate's get-up was brand-new and Ralph Lauren all the way, while Phoebe's was vintage and only borderline seaworthy. Hillary was wearing high-tech but well-used Patagonia gear. She optimistically grabbed her wraparound sunglasses, and everyone brought either a visor or a baseball hat, and a fleece or windbreaker.

Down in the kitchen, Gee was already at the long, wooden table with the newspaper spread out before her. A mug of hot coffee and a plate of buttered rye toast sat to one side and her reading glasses were perched low on her nose. Her hair was still damp at the ends from her morning swim.

"Good morning, my little chickadees! Are you excited for sailing clinic?" she asked, peering over the rims of her glasses.

"I'm psyched!" said Hillary enthusiastically. Phoebe just grunted.

They grabbed plates and spooned on some warm scrambled eggs, adding a couple of slices of bacon each, and mini corn muffins with strawberry jam. Then they sat on the banquette to quickly eat before they raced out the door.

"Yummy breakfast, Sheila. Thanks!" said Kate appreciatively.

Sheila had appeared with the coffeepot in her hand. She spoke matter-of-factly in her sandpapery voice. "Ya need yer strength out there on the water, to be sure." She refilled Gee's cup and reluctantly offered some to Neeve, too. "Ya know, where I'm from, it's bad luck for women to go out in boats. The fishermen won't allow it. Been that way for centuries."

The girls exchanged glances. Neeve was puzzled. "I lived there for years and I never heard any of that."

"But you were on the mainland, weren't you lass? Out in the Blasket Islands, and Dingle, where my people are from, the customs are old and they're there for a reason. Women belong on land, where they can be safe and tend to their elders and the young'uns. Oh, I could tell yas stories about girls that went traipsing out to sea . . ."

"Yes, dear Sheila, I'm sure you could," Gee interrupted brightly, as she looked around the table at the girls' worried faces. Kate, especially, looked like she was going to be sick.

"But these girls need to get off to *sailing clinic* right now, so let's not add any worries to weigh them down, alrighty?" She gave Sheila a meaningful look.

"Yes, Mrs. Callahan," said Sheila, catching Gee's drift. "Of course. For another time then. I'm off to do the washing, now. Good luck to yas!"

"Girls, I don't want any of you to feel scared of sailing, but we'll need to set out some rules if you're planning to be out sailing without any adults." Gee glanced at the delicate gold watch on her wrist. "Unfortunately, I've got to run now, but we can discuss this later. Give it some thought. Kisses!" And she dashed off to church, leaving the girls with eager entreaties to tell her all about sailing clinic that night at dinner.

In the silence that followed, the girls stopped chewing and looked at one another.

"Do you think she knows?" asked Hillary, raising her eyebrows.

"Nah," said Neeve over the rim of her coffee cup. "No way."

When they reached Hagan's, a small crowd of kids had already lined up at the door to the marina building, waiting to go into the lounge area. The cousins coasted up to the bike rack, stashed their red bikes, grabbed their bags, and headed over to join the patient group of young sailors. Sloan was nowhere to be seen, and this made the girls relax a bit, though they were still wary of her impending arrival.

Inside, they sat in a big room with a cathedral ceiling and

one huge, plate glass wall that looked out on the water. Mr. Hagan, a tall, thin man in his sixties with a gray crew cut and a dazzling white smile, stood in front of the window facing the kids; with him were the rest of the counselors, guys and girls ranging in age from their late teens to early twenties. He gave a little speech about safety and then he introduced the instructors, who all seemed nice.

"Okay, Mrs. Hagan is giving me the long-winded old man signal." Everyone laughed and turned to look at Mrs. Hagan, who was pretending to grab a hook and haul Mr. Hagan offstage. "So let's get down to business and divide you into your groups," said Mr. Hagan.

The girls were quickly placed into Tucker's beginner group with two other kids (Hillary fudged the truth a little about her own experience, just so she could stay with the cousins). They were all happily chatting when Sloan sauntered in. She passed them on her way to check in with Mr. Hagan.

"Poor Tuck. You've got the beginners!" she said in a fakesweet voice. "Won't you be bored?"

Neeve stared daggers at her, and the others exchanged uneasy glances.

Tucker was momentarily flustered by her rudeness as well, but then he recovered. "I was lucky enough to get the nicest group here, and since I'm such a great instructor, they won't be beginners for long!" He laughed and winked at the Callahans, then turned his back on Sloan dismissively.

She pouted and continued over to Mr. Hagan, who assigned her to the "expert" group. But Hillary had an unsettling sense of being stared at all morning, and whenever she glanced at Sloan's "expert" group, Sloan was quickly looking away from her, as if she'd been staring. *Whatever,* thought Hillary at first. *At least she's not in our actual group. It would be horrible to be stuck in such close quarters with your enemy all day.* But later, out of the blue, a memory popped into Hillary's head.

She had been about four or five years old, sitting in church with her parents, and a little girl her age kept turning around from the pew in front of them and staring at her. It had bugged Hillary to no end, and she kept staring right back. Finally, Hillary had called her mother's attention to the problem and her mother had whispered distractedly, "Just smile at her and say hi." Hillary had thought her mother was crazy for a moment, but then — probably out of frustration — she'd tried it. And the girl had smiled back. They spent the rest of the mass whispering back and forth and were fast friends at Sunday school from then on. The sudden arrival of this memory confused Hillary and she tried to put it out of her mind. Sloan wasn't like Maude, the girl at church. She was mean and she definitely did not want to be their friend. Right?

Over the course of the morning, the Callahans had a hilarious time with Tucker. The other kids in their group — an eleven-year-old boy named Atticus, a funny smart-aleck who looked a little like Huckleberry Finn (as Phoebe pointed out), and his buddy Cal — were fun, too. To Hillary, the best part of clinic was that by the end of the morning, Phoebe and Kate already seemed more comfortable with the idea of going sailing, even though they didn't have a chance to go out this first day.

Phoebe admitted it, too. "Knowledge is power," she declared. And Hillary agreed.

After clinic, the girls had lunch in town, then rode over to the library. Phoebe had been eager to continue their search for all things Callahan, and they'd agreed that they should get moving on finding their maps, as well.

The first thing that struck Hillary about the Gull Island Public Library was the smell — it made her feel like she was going back in time. The old, gluey, musty, moldy smell was somehow very pleasant, even though Hillary really wasn't a book person. The small brick building had tall shelves of books and periodicals that filled the basement and ground floor levels, while the attic had been turned into a sunny loft for children, with low shelves of kids' books and comfy armchairs and bean bags to flop on. The girls toured through the whole building, looking for the head librarian, Mrs. Merrihew, before they finally found her in the little yard out back, weeding through boxes of donated books someone had just dropped off. A lawnmower buzzed at the house next door and the sweet, tickly smell of freshly mown grass hung over the library's backyard.

"Hello girls," she said, straightening back up and putting

her hands on her rather stout hips. She was an older woman, short and thickly set, but spry and capable-looking, like a gym teacher. Her frosted blondish hair was set into a helmet of immobilized curls that made her look as if she had just spent the morning at the beauty parlor with a bunch of old ladies, but her gray eyes sparkled merrily and radiated laugh lines.

"Hi, Mrs. Merrihew," Phoebe began. "These are my cousins Neeve, Kate, and Hillary. We've come to see you because we need to try to locate an island in the sound and we thought you might be able to help us."

"Yes, indeedy. A search beats sorting books any day." Mrs. Merrihew dusted her hands off on her skirt and stepped over the piles of books she had arranged. "Follow me inside and we'll sit down and have a chat." She paused to look at them again and said, "My, you girls all look alike — save for the hair, of course. You've all got your grandmother's eyes!"

"That's what they tell us!" said Neeve, as if this was old news. But Hillary beamed. Without any siblings of her own, these resemblance comments were rare for her and she loved feeling part of the tribe.

The girls followed the bustling Mrs. Merrihew inside to a small conference room where they could sit and talk without disturbing any other library patrons. Through an unspoken agreement, the girls naturally deferred to Phoebe in the library. It was her turf.

When they were all seated, Phoebe began to explain. She filled Mrs. Merrihew in on their two quests: the search for

Callahan family crest and motto information, and their hunt for a particular island in the sound where their dads used to go. Mrs. Merrihew must've wondered what they were up to, but she didn't ask. Instead, she just nodded quietly, making notes on a legal pad as Phoebe talked, and occasionally asking a question. When Phoebe finished, Mrs. Merrihew sat back and thoughtfully reviewed her notes, biting the top of her pen while she read.

"I like this. This is a good, meaty hunt. Let me run and grab a few things and I'll be back in a jiffy."

"Great. Thank you so much," gushed Phoebe, who was excited to begin. Mrs. Merrihew bustled out the door.

Hillary felt vaguely nauseated by the idea of being stuck indoors, poring over old documents for hours on a beautiful afternoon. This was starting to feel a little like school, which was probably why Phoebe was so happy.

Ten minutes later, Mrs. Merrihew breezed back in like a breath of fresh air; in her arms was a stack of books, some very large.

"Okay, I found a few things to get you started," she began. "Do you girls know how to read charts?"

"No, ma'm, not really," admitted Phoebe.

Mrs. Merrihew pointed things out as she gave them a cursory lesson. "Alrighty, since water depths and the shapes of these sandy islands can fluctuate over time, you're better off using the old tidal chart to figure out which island your dads used to go to. Now, I picked this other chart book from 1970 because it would have the chart your fathers would have been likely to use; this next survey wasn't done until 1985. So you can just compare that old chart against this new chart to see if things look the same or different out there today."

Phoebe glanced down at her notebook in excitement. "You guys! That must've been what Talbot was about to tell us when Sloan chased him off the other day. He was telling us to compare something, because tidal islands change shape over time. Cool! That had been bugging me. Thanks, Mrs. Merrihew!"

The librarian smiled. "Glad to be of service. Now, why don't you look through these charts, flag the relevant pages, and then copy them when you're ready to leave. Meanwhile, take a look at this tidal almanac to figure out when the full moons are. Full moons cause spring tides, which you'll need to plan for. Also, I've brought two Irish history books, and one of them has a section on family names and the other has a section on crests, so you might find something there."

"What are these spring tides everyone keeps talking about?" asked Hillary.

"Oh my," began Mrs. Merrihew. "I'm afraid I'm in a bit over my head with that one, if you'll pardon the pun." She giggled girlishly at her own joke. "All I know is what I've told you. You're going to have to get a real sailor to explain it."

"Okay," said Hillary. Talbot or Tucker could probably help them with that.

"Thanks, Mrs. Merrihew!" said Neeve.

"It's the least I can do for the Callahans. Your family has

been so good to this library. Especially your grandmother. Now if you need me, I'll be out back, sifting through sandy old paperbacks. Ta-ta!" And she left.

The girls divided up the materials and eagerly set to work; all was quiet for a few moments as they got their bearings.

Suddenly Phoebe pounded her fist on the table and everyone jumped.

"Look!" She held up her book and pointed at one family crest on a page featuring a dozen or so.

The others peered across the table. "Cool! You found our crest!" enthused Kate, reading the family name under the picture.

Hillary rose to inspect the crest. It was shaped like a shield and showed a fox coming out of a bunch of trees. Underneath, it said "Fidus et Audax." *Whatever that means, I hope it's something good,* thought Hillary.

After studying it for a moment, Hillary looked up. "How can we figure out what the picture in this crest means and what the words underneath it are?"

Phoebe pulled the other heavy book toward her and did a little cross-referencing. "The fox — which represents cleverness — is emerging from a grove of oaks, which represents strength."

"Brilliant!" cried Neeve.

"And the motto, which is in Latin, means 'faithful and bold,'" Phoebe continued.

"Excellent!" Hillary grinned. "Just like us! Well, some of us," she teased.

"It's great stuff for our flag," added Kate, turning the book toward her. "And it will be pretty easy to reproduce the picture."

"Great job, Bee." Hillary returned to her maps. She had located the two charts in the current Rhode Island survey that corresponded to Gull Island. She couldn't begin to follow what the map said — and none of the islands looked just like Gull — so she just flagged it to copy and bring home. Then she turned to the older map and looked for the same pages. And she looked, and she looked.

"That's weird . . . ," she said.

"What?" Kate raised her head from the pages she was flagging in the almanac.

Hillary flipped back and forth again, then she examined the page numbers. Sure enough, just as she had begun to suspect: There were two pages missing. Torn out.

"Bummer!" she said in frustration. "Someone ripped out two pages from this old map book. Now we'll never find out what the islands looked like when our dads were kids!"

You would've thought someone had been shot, the way Phoebe reacted, thought Hillary later. "Someone ripped a book!" Phoebe cried in alarm. "What is this world coming to? Oh, you just know it was that little Bicket weasel, don't you? She's just the type to rip a book!"

Hillary wasn't sure, but she was upset about the missing pages. Even a non-scholar like her knew that it would be really hard to find something with the out-of-date information they needed.

Meanwhile, Kate had finished diligently flagging pages in the almanac, and the girls realized they could now make their copies and go home to review them.

The late afternoon sunlight poured over the island like golden honey as they pedaled back to The Sound. The ferry had just arrived with a larger crop of cars and people than usual. Summer visitors were starting to arrive and the roads were getting busier. Along the way, they saw numerous cars pulled over at the farm stands, stocking up on fresh food for the week, and they knew that the quiet period on the island was ending. Soon, vacationers would arrive and stay for weeks at a time: The beach would be packed, the water would be busy with boats, and the donuts at the News Co. would start to sell out earlier.

But the girls could feel things calming down again when they passed the Little Store and waved at Farren, who was outside chatting with a friend. North Wing wasn't tourist territory, no matter what Sloan said.

After dinner that night, as they lay around Neeve and Kate's room in layers of homemade moisturizing face masks, Kate wondered aloud why they didn't just e-mail their dads and ask them where the island was.

Hillary sat up quickly from where she was lying on the floor and peeled two cucumber slices off her eyes. "Because that would give away the surprise of it all!" she cried. "We can't just ask them! Then they'll all get talking and forbid us from doing it or something. We have to do it on our own. Prove we're worthy of the Callahan name!"

"I agree," said Neeve firmly. "It's all about the surprise. They'll be so shocked when we tell them we've actually done it."

"When *are* we going to do it, anyway?" asked Phoebe. "We've got less than two weeks left." Phoebe seemed to be moving away from the dread of doing it and into the resigned mode of just getting it over with.

Hillary had been thinking about this, too. "I figure we need the better part of a day to do it. Any of these little islands is going to take, like, two hours to sail to and two hours back, plus maybe an hour when we're actually there."

"So the only full days we have are weekends, since we can't bag clinic," said Kate, clearly hoping someone would suggest they do just that.

No one took the bait. "That actually means it has to be either this Saturday or Sunday," said Phoebe, gently touching her mask to make sure she hadn't cracked it by talking.

They were silent a minute while they thought about this. There was so much to do before then. Find a map, fix the boat, figure out the tide times, make the flag. Finally Kate spoke up in a small voice. "Did you guys hear what Gee said at dinner tonight? She has to go onto the mainland on Sunday for a baby shower for some relative of Pops'." Kate seemed reluctant to share this information, as if she knew Hillary and Neeve would seize that as the day to sail.

"I think she wanted us to volunteer to go with her," said Neeve wistfully; she clearly would relish such a social event.

"I think that's when we'll have to go," said Hillary at last.

"With only six days left, we've got quite a task ahead of us," announced Phoebe, stating the obvious.

CHAPTER THIRTEEN

Let's Get to Work

After clinic on Tuesday, the girls raced back to The Sound to work on the boat. They wolfed down their lunch, then ran upstairs and grabbed the boat-fixing supplies to head down to Gee's tiny boathouse. Neeve had arranged for Tucker to come over around five for dinner that night, so the girls knew they'd have a somewhat expert opinion of their work at day's end, but Hillary realized she had better put in a quick call to Smitty, too. She sent the others ahead down to the boat, and stopped in the kitchen to dial the boat shop. After Sloan's comments about Smitty's memory, Hillary was surprised to find that he remembered his promised house call. He said he'd stop by to give the boat a once-over on Friday afternoon; Hillary just hoped he'd remember to come. As they hung up, though, Smitty made a strange request.

"Tell Sheila to make me up a big batch of her famous

scones, alright?" Hillary could practically hear his mouth watering over the phone.

"Okay . . . ," Hillary agreed, confused. Sheila walked into the kitchen just as Hillary was hanging up the phone.

Hillary stood for a moment with her hand on the receiver. *How does Smitty know Sheila and her scones so well?* she wondered.

"Sheila," Hillary began. "That was Smithson Bicket on the phone. He's coming to look at our boat, I mean Gee's boat, on Friday, and he asked for some scones. Do you know what he means?"

Sheila had just started polishing silver at the sink, so her back was to Hillary. Hillary heard her snort, though, and laugh a dry laugh.

"I'll have 'em ready. Need to make two dozen of 'em, though, the way that lad eats." Sheila laughed again and shook her head.

Strange, thought Hillary, but she didn't press the subject because she didn't want Sheila to end up asking her all kinds of questions about the boat and why they were fixing it. So she thanked Sheila and jogged down to find the others. She relayed the conversation, and the others agreed that Smitty and Sheila must just know each other from living on the same island for years. Hillary shrugged it off and they set to work.

There was much grunting and groaning as the girls tried to drag the boat outside. Finally, they managed to get it lugged slightly up off the rocks of Gee's beach, remove the mast, and prop the boat upside down on two sawhorses that Hillary had dashed to the garage to fetch.

"Okay," Phoebe began, peering over her notes from their meeting with Smitty. "First thing is the fine-grain sandpaper. Do we have it?"

"Check," said Hillary.

"Alright. First we sand the outside." Phoebe laid the notebook aside, and each girl took up a sheet of sandpaper. "We don't need to remove *all* the paint, we just need to remove any barnacles or bubbles and make the surface smooth so it can absorb new paint."

"You got it, sister," said Neeve, who was wearing a bikini and a straw cowboy hat. She tipped her hat at Phoebe and began to sand.

Hillary tied her lucky bandanna around her head to keep her hair out of her eyes, then she joined in. The girls were tentative at first, but as they realized how much power was needed, they began to really work, and eventually started belting out songs just to get a rhythm going for the sanding.

Hillary got the gang rolling first with a version of her school's cheer, adapted for their circumstances. "We are the Callahans, the mighty, mighty Callahans, and everywhere we go . . . People want to know . . . Who we are, so we tell them . . . We are the Callahans, the mighty, mighty Callahans, and everywhere we go . . ." and so on. The others enjoyed this for a while, and Neeve even developed a little dance routine around it, where she'd spin at a certain part and then clap her hands back onto the hull of the boat. Then they all took turns adapting songs to their own family name, with each one sillier than the last. Kate changed the "Sesame Street" theme song to

"Gee's House," as in, "Can you tell me how to get, how to get to Gee's house?" And Phoebe, ever the hippie, threw in "Blue-Eyed Girl," the Callahan version of the old Van Morrison song "Brown-Eyed Girl."

But Neeve took the cake when she started singing the Singapore national anthem in Chinese at first, then in English. She changed the word "Singapore" to "Callahans," and sang "Onward Callahans! Onward Callahans!" The girls doubled over with laughter — partially from hearing Neeve singing in Chinese and partially from watching her, for she was delivering the song in mock earnestness, with her eyes closed and her hat removed and respectfully held to her chest.

The laughter and songs subsided shortly thereafter, as the girls' hands began cramping and blistering from the sanding. Just when they thought they couldn't go on, Hillary announced a surprise inspection and decided they were in pretty good shape. They were ready to reseal the cracks in the hull.

The caulking gun was sort of hard to use at first, but Phoebe finally insisted on reading the directions, and then she figured it out. They'd bought two putty knives, so people traded turns and they laboriously resealed every crack on the hull. While the caulk dried in the late afternoon sun, the girls dashed up the hill for a swim. The fumes from the caulk had made them kind of giddy and they all started talking like pirates while they swam and dove.

"Aaargh, mateys!" cried Hillary as she cannonballed into the pool.

"Avast, me hearties!" echoed Neeve, doing a perfect backward dive off the edge.

No one heard Tucker, at first, as he called to them from the terrace.

Kate was pretending to walk the plank when they finally noticed him. They were embarrassed that he'd found them acting so immaturely, but they waved him down to the pool and were relieved to find he was amused by their antics. He tactfully explained that he had to escape the Bicket house after being under Sloan's thumb all afternoon, so he'd ridden his bike over early. The girls sobered quickly at the mention of Sloan's name, and Neeve started grilling Tucker about the Bicket family.

"Whoa, whoa, whoa!" protested Tucker, at last, raising his hands as if to protect himself from the onslaught of Neeve's interrogation. "Why are you all so interested in each other, anyway?"

"Oh, no special reason," said Neeve, trying unsuccessfully to affect a casual air.

"What do you mean, each other?" asked Phoebe, her eyes narrowing suspiciously. "Does Sloan ask about us?"

"All the time!" cried Tucker. "She was furious that I was coming over here for dinner. I thought you all didn't even know each other, but now I'm getting bombarded by questions from both sides! What's the deal? Clue me in!"

"Hmm. Interesting," said Phoebe, crossing her arms. "Sloan asks about *us*."

Hillary was quickly reminded of how Sloan had stared at them that first day in clinic. It had been like she was longing to be a part of their group — and not just because of Tucker. Hillary shook her head to clear the thought, then she glanced at the others. "Well, if you really want to know the story . . . ," she began. No one stopped her, so while Tucker listened quietly, she related their flag-planting plan, and all of the history between the Callahans and the Bickets.

Tucker nodded when Hillary finished. "It sounds like the Hatfields and the McCoys!" he said with a grin.

"That's what I think!" said Phoebe. "But no one here reads any books, let alone any Mark Twain, so I never mentioned it!" She beamed at Tucker in gratitude.

"Whatever," said Neeve with a dismissive wave of her hand.

"I read!" protested Kate.

"*Crafts Quarterly* doesn't count," snapped Phoebe. But then she saw the wounded look on Kate's face and apologized.

"So what does Sloan ask about us?" asked Neeve, her eyes narrowing.

"Oh, the same kinds of things you ask," said Tucker. "What are they up to? Are they jerks? Why do you hang out with them? What kind of boat do they have? Stuff like that."

"Are *we* jerks?!" Neeve was indignant. "Talk about the pot calling the kettle black!"

"Listen, this is a waste of our time," interrupted Hillary. "Let's get Tucker to come look at the boat and see what he thinks, and then let's show him the stuff from the library, okay?"

Everyone agreed and they trooped back down to the boat. Tucker was laughingly surprised at first by the messiness of the work they'd done and by their excessive use of caulk ("It's not cake frosting!" he had laughed), but he ventured that the boat was probably totally watertight at this point.

"You know it's supposed to rain for the next couple of days, right?" he asked.

The girls were caught off-guard. "Nooo . . . ," said Hillary.

"I think you need to get this paint on now, at least the first coat. Do you want me to help you?" asked Tucker.

"Yes, let's do it," said Neeve.

They shook the two heavy cans of green boat paint, and Tucker pried them open with his Swiss Army knife. Then Tucker, Phoebe, Neeve, and Hillary grabbed brushes while Kate gave artistic direction. The paint went on quickly, if sloppily, but when they'd finished the coat, the boat really looked wonderful. Refreshed. They left it to dry, trudged back up the hill, deposited Tucker in the kitchen with Sheila, and then ran upstairs to change for dinner. Gee would be home any minute, so the map review would have to wait.

Dinner was a huge success. Tucker amused them all with stories of captaining his sailing team at boarding school, and various summer sailing adventures in Maine. He and Gee got on like a house on fire, and the girls were thrilled they'd had him over.

After dinner, Gee went to return phone calls in her room — although it was clear that she actually felt she should just leave the "young people" to themselves for a while. So the girls and Tucker took the opportunity to review their sailing plan for Sunday.

Tucker spread the maps and almanac pages out on the library floor once more. Phoebe sat on the ottoman, poised with her pen and notebook, and the others clustered around Tucker and the materials.

"Okay," he began. "I know you still need to double check all this against an old chart, but I'm guessing that this is the island you're thinking of right here." He pointed to a tiny island in the sound, not far offshore, that was vaguely shaped like a small flying gull, if you squinted. It was labeled "Quocasset," but underneath that name, in tiny italic script, it said *"Little Gull Island."*

Hillary nodded as she absently spun her rope bracelet on her wrist. "Yeah. That would make sense. It looks kind of like a seagull. I'm not gonna get too excited yet, though. We still need to confirm it."

Tucker leaned forward and picked up an almanac page. "Good. The full moon isn't until next week. That means the spring tide won't be running."

"Everyone keeps mentioning this spring tide like it's this big, dreaded thing and I still don't know what it is! What would it mean for us?" asked Phoebe, looking up from the notebook in frustration.

"It's nothing dangerous," Tucker assured them. "You'd just need to find out the high and low tide times for that day. You'd want to sail out as the tide is going out — low tide. And come back as the tide is coming in — high tide. The spring tide just exaggerates the tides — so the high is really high and the low is really low, and the currents will flow really strong in the channels around these little islands. You don't want to get caught trying to go against the tide because it's really tough going."

"Is it really that powerful?" asked Kate, anxiously biting her lip.

"Yes, but you'd just need to be smart about it. You'd leave here on time, and you wouldn't dawdle out there. If you got caught out there in a low tide, you might run aground. Then you'd be stuck for a while, which would be a hassle and might even damage the bottom of your newly beautiful boat out there." Tucker winked at Kate.

"Phew. At least we don't have to worry about that!" said Kate.

"So how should we go?" asked Neeve.

Tucker looked at the charts for a minute and thought. "If it were me, I'd go this way, then over here . . ." He pointed out a route and Phoebe leaned in and traced it in blue pen right onto the Xeroxed chart.

When he'd finished, Tucker stood up and stretched. He looked at his watch. "I think I'd better get going so you girls can get some sleep. Thank you so much for that great dinner and all the fun. It was really nice to be over here — it was nice to have a change of scenery, even though the Bickets aren't as bad as you think."

"Humph!" said Neeve.

The girls gathered up their papers and Phoebe took them to put with the notebook. They walked Tucker slowly back to the kitchen because he wanted to thank Sheila for dinner and say goodbye to her, too.

As he climbed onto his bike outside, he paused. "You know, I have to warn you, I think Sloan is planning on heading out there soon, too."

Phoebe groaned. "That's all we need. To run into her on the high seas!"

"Just as long as we get our flag in there first, so we can show her who's boss," said Neeve with her chin in the air.

Tucker laughed and was off, wobbling down the crunchy driveway.

"Yeah, and then we've gotta make sure it's *still* in there when our dads come," added Hillary quietly. All she could think of these days was the look on her dad's face when they sailed out to the island and he saw the flag. That was all she cared about.

CHAPTER FOURTEEN

Tea Time

$\mathscr{A}$ll through clinic on Wednesday, Hillary kept glancing at the sky. Tucker finally teased her about it. "Are you expecting visitors from outer space?"

"Nah, just hoping it won't rain before we can get another coat of paint on the boat." She watched as the sky went from hazy and white, to overcast, to cloudy. She just prayed it wouldn't actually rain before they could get the things done that they needed to.

As soon as the noon whistle blew, the girls tumbled out of Hagan's and onto their bikes. Hillary insisted they ride home first, get the boat back into the shed, and try to get one more coat of paint onto it, even if that meant the rain came before they could get back into town for flag-making supplies from the Old Mill.

Back home, dark clouds were threatening on the horizon, so the girls ditched their boat bags in the kitchen, raced past a bewildered Sheila with just a wave, and ran down the backyard to the boat. With much effort, they lugged the boat back to its shed, and Kate grabbed the sawhorses so they could keep the boat on them, hull-side up.

It was tight inside the shed, so Kate and Neeve, being the smallest, slid in to apply the final coat of paint. Hillary and Phoebe stood outside as fat drops of rain began to fall from the leaden clouds above; then they called to the others that they'd meet them inside, and they beat a hasty retreat to Sheila's egg salad sandwiches in the kitchen.

When Neeve and Kate returned from the shed, they were woozy from the paint fumes and everything was funny. Sheila pretended to be annoyed by their antics, but Hillary caught her smiling as she served them their lunch, and she knew Sheila was getting a kick out of them.

That's how she got the courage to ask, "Sheila, is there any way you could drive us to town after lunch? Since it's Gee's day to volunteer at the Health Clinic, and it's pouring rain, we don't have any other way of getting there, or I wouldn't ask you."

Four smiling faces turned to Sheila in hope, and Sheila privately put her afternoon plan of airing out the linen closet on hold. "A'course," she agreed. "I could do some errands meself."

"Thanks!" said the girls gratefully. And Sheila went upstairs to change into her "town clothes."

"I have an idea," said Neeve with a twinkle in her eye. "Why don't *we* change into town clothes?!"

"Oh no, here we go," moaned Phoebe. "What are 'town clothes,' Neeve?" But Hillary could tell Phoebe was starting to admit to herself how much she enjoyed Neeve's imaginative and wild streak. It certainly made her life more interesting.

"Well, whatever you like!" said Neeve innocently. "But I'm thinking of wearing that old ball gown we found up in the attic; you know, the one with the bustle? I'll have to rig up something with that hem, 'cause it's so long on me. That and Hillary's cowboy boots. And maybe my cowboy hat. Hmm, what to do with my hair?" she pondered.

Hillary laughed. *Leave it to Neeve to bring style to a boring errand,* she thought. "I'll wear your tutu, Neeve, if it'll fit me."

"But of course, madam," said Neeve with a smile. "And now for you two, the wicked stepsisters?" she cackled at Phoebe and Kate's frowns. "What can we find for Drusilla and Esmerelda?"

"Oh, alright," said Kate in capitulation. "I just don't want to run into anyone I know, is all." Phoebe nodded in agreement.

One hour and many outfit changes later, the girls were ensconced in their "chariot" (also known as Sheila's ancient Wagoneer) on their way to town. Neeve was pretending to be a queen, waving at the throngs of imaginary well-wishers, her loyal subjects, lining the sides of Fisher's Path.

Kate hadn't been into it until Neeve had dug the tiara out of Gee's party supply cache, and then she'd perked right up. Contrary to Phoebe's assertion that she didn't read, Kate was a huge fan of *The Princess Diaries*. And Phoebe, the most reluctant participant of all, looked smashing in an ancient kimono, with full geisha makeup applied by Neeve herself: white face, red cheeks, red lips, and tons of eye shadow. Phoebe was comforted by the fact that no one would recognize her. The others didn't point out that it would be hard to miss her — even in a low bun, her white-blonde hair was most un-geisha-like and very distinctive — but no one wanted a cranky Phoebe on her hands.

Sheila dropped them off at the Old Mill, and Neeve announced they'd be done in about an hour and a half. Sheila had plenty of errands to do, but the others were puzzled. What would take them so long? They only had a few things to buy — fabric markers and paint and maybe some while sailcloth. But Neeve had another plan up her sleeve: afternoon tea at the Coolidge House Hotel.

After completing their transactions at the Old Mill, Neeve led the procession across Broad Street to the tall, brick Coolidge House. The other girls had finally lost their self-consciousness; Neeve's infectious enthusiasm had overpowered their cowardice. So by the time they were all seated in the antique-filled Coolidge House parlor, under the amused and indulgent eye of the maître d', the girls were having a blast.

The waiter really hammed it up, too, since they were basically his only customers on this soggy, midweek afternoon. He brought them a wide selection of sweets and tiny sandwiches "on the house," and poured their tea with a flourish and lots of bowing. The girls giggled and stuck out their pinkies to drink from the delicate china cups, even though every single one of them hated hot tea.

By the time they had to go meet Sheila, François, the waiter, was their new best friend (his real name was Frankie, but Neeve had changed it to suit the occasion). They air-kissed him goodbye, and with one last sweep of Kate's scraggly feather boa, they departed.

They went to stand on the small, covered front porch of the Old Mill to wait for Sheila, but she was running late. The rain started to come down again, and Hillary hopped off the porch to take a long look up the road to see if she could see Sheila's Wagoneer approaching. Just as she turned to go back, a gray pickup truck slowed to a halt beside her, its wheels sizzling on the wet pavement. The passenger's side window cranked down and there was Talbot, grinning at her. "Need a ride, um, ballerina lady?"

Hillary laughed, embarrassed to be caught in such a get-up, but happy to see Talbot. "We're just waiting for our ride, actually, but thanks. I don't want to ditch her or she'll go crazy looking for us." She took a peek at the driver, who must've been Talbot's dad. "Hi." She smiled.

"Oh, I'm sorry, this is my dad, Truman St. John. Dad, this is Hillary Callahan, one of the famous Callahan cousins."

Mr. St. John was a burly teddy bear of a man with a shiny, shaved head. He smiled a huge, kind grin. "It's nice to meet you. I'm sorry you're stuck out there in the rain."

"Oh, that's okay," said Hillary. Suddenly Phoebe called to her from the porch. "What?" Hillary called back. She couldn't hear her.

Phoebe ducked out of the porch and ran to the street, her head bent to avoid the rain. When she reached the car, Talbot laughed but quickly contained himself. He put his hands together and bowed his head in greeting.

"Very funny," said Phoebe wryly. "Hi," she said to Talbot's dad, and the introductions were made again. "Listen, Mr. St. John, I just was wondering . . . Um, this is so random, but my cousins and I are looking for an old, out-of-date chart, and I wondered if you might have a copy of it lying around somewhere?"

Hillary smacked her own forehead. "Of course! What a brilliant idea, Bee!"

"No problem," said Mr. St. John. "What are you looking for?"

Phoebe explained and Mr. St. John nodded his head slowly. "I actually might have what you're looking for. When I bought my boat last year, the guy who sold it to me gave me all of his old charts and things. They're back at the house, but I can look and if I find it, I'll have Talbot get it to you girls."

Hillary was impressed. It was so easy! Why hadn't they thought of Talbot's dad before? They smiled and thanked Mr.

St. John, and just then, Hillary saw Sheila's headlights approaching. She waved Neeve and Kate down from the porch and said goodbye to Talbot and his dad.

Back at the house, the girls set up camp in the sewing room. Hillary channel-surfed while Neeve made a beaded necklace, Phoebe cut up old magazines for a word collage for her best friend back home, and Kate worked out the flag design on paper before committing it to the sailcloth.

Hillary wasn't allowed to watch much television at home. Her parents were as active and athletic as she was, so they usually went outside and kicked a soccer ball around when they had down time. Right now, though, Hillary was enjoying the mindlessness of the dumb shows that were on, and thinking about her parents. Or her dad, to be more specific.

She'd always worried that her dad had really wanted a son. He was such a huge sports fan, and he loved to camp and go whitewater rafting, and all kinds of macho stuff. Hillary was never sure if she'd gotten into all that because it was fun, or because she wanted to please her dad and make up for the fact that she wasn't a boy. She knew he would deny to the ends of the earth that he'd wanted a son — he always said how much he loved having a daughter and what a great daughter Hillary was. But since the separation, Hillary hadn't been able to shake the feeling that her dad had cast the "womenfolk" aside and struck out on his own. Maybe, she thought, if she'd been a boy, she could have gone with him. It would've been kind of an adventure: the Callahans united against the world.

"There," said Kate, interrupting Hillary's thoughts. "I think I've got it." She held the drawing up for everyone to inspect. It was a horizontal rectangle. Across the top it said CALLAHAN in bold letters. In the middle was a simple line drawing version of their crest, and beneath it, it said "Fidus et Audax" in fancy script.

"I love it!" whooped Neeve.

Hillary leaned in to see better. "It's awesome, Katie. Thank you." It looked really cool. Hillary's stomach fluttered in anticipation of the day her dad would see it.

"So now you paint this on?" asked Phoebe.

"Uh-huh. I think I should get some newspaper to put under it, though." She looked uneasily at the golden sisal rug that covered the wood floor.

And sure enough, half an hour later, as Kate was shifting one of the jars of red paint, it overturned. It was only a split second before she caught it, but a dribble of the paint had poured onto the rug, in the only spot where there was no newspaper drop cloth.

"Aaargh!" shouted Kate. "Look what I did!"

The others jumped up to inspect the accidental damage. The paint had formed a puddle about two inches in diameter.

"Bummer," said Phoebe quietly.

Hillary ran to get paper towels. "What kind of paint is it?" she asked when she returned with the roll.

"Well, it's fabric paint. So it's not made to come out easily," admitted Kate.

They mopped it up as best they could, and then decided they'd better go find Sheila. In their haste, they forgot to hide the flag.

Moments later, as they filed into the room with Sheila in the lead, the girls realized their mistake. "What's this, then?" asked Sheila, more interested in the flag than the stain.

"Oh, um . . . just a little . . ." Kate could never bring herself to lie, especially to a grown-up. She looked wide-eyed at the others for help, but they were speechless, too.

"It's our flag," Neeve stated flatly. There was nothing else to do but admit it.

"I thought ya'd put that outer yer minds," said Sheila. "It's not a happy business, that." She put her fists on her hips and looked at them. "I tell yas, I'm more bothered about ya gettin' all mixed up in this flag shenanigans than the stain. The stain I can lift with some a'that OxiClean and detergent, but the flag . . ." She shook her head. "You don't want to do anything that can't be undone."

The girls were silent.

"I think you should have a talk with yer grandmother about yer plan," said Sheila finally. "It's not up to me to forbid yas, but . . ."

"Please don't tell Gee!" whispered Neeve fervently. "We need to do this. For Hillary's sake!"

Everyone turned to look at Hillary. *Boy,* thought Hillary. *This divorce thing is sure coming in handy!* She made her eyes look sad and needy and stared at Sheila like a puppy dog who wants a home.

Sheila blew out an exasperated blast of air, but the puppy dog thing was definitely working on her. "I don't know what all this is about. But it's not my business to tattle on yas to yer grandmother, unless it's an emergency. I just think ya should tell her yerself before you go startin' things up. See what she says about it!" She turned on her heel to get the cleaning supplies and the girls looked at each other — half in dismay that they'd been found out, and half-pleased that the Hillary excuse had saved them for the time being.

"I still don't think we should tell Gee until it's a fact," whispered Neeve. "Why get her all worked up unless it's really happening?"

Kate was skeptical. "Wouldn't it just be easier to tell her?"

"And have her forbid us? No way!" said Hillary in a quiet voice. She knew Kate hoped that exactly that would happen.

Phoebe was pensive. "We've got to be more careful or Gee's definitely going to start putting two and two together. The boat, maps, a flag. What else could she think?"

Hillary smiled gratefully at Phoebe. "I'll be in charge of secrecy," she offered. "I'll keep all the stuff hidden. The boat, well, we just need her to think we want to practice all the new things we're learning at clinic, and go out on sails for picnics and stuff, okay?"

Neeve nodded her head. "And that's all true."

"It's only for a couple more days, anyway," said Hillary rationally. She watched as Kate caved.

"Okay," Kate finally said. "Whatever you say."

CHAPTER FIFTEEN

Ship Shape

Clinic was canceled on Thursday because of the rain. Kate and Phoebe were elated, partially because they weren't crazy about sailing and partially because they loved indoor, rainy-day activities. But Hillary and Neeve were restless.

After breakfast, Kate announced that she had a secret project she was working on. The others were intrigued, but they couldn't pry any information out of her. She disappeared for an hour and everyone else wandered into the sewing room — where the red paint stain had been reduced to a pale pink splash by Sheila, who assured them it would fade over time from the sun — and hung out in their pajamas.

Gee wandered in and saw the new stain on the rug. Hillary apologized and admitted that some paint had spilled and Sheila had helped to clean it up. But she quickly changed the subject before Gee could ask any questions.

"Gee, do you have any great ideas of things for us to do to-day?" she asked.

Gee offered to take them to the whaling museum in town when Kate returned, and they all agreed. But later, as she thought back on it, Hillary realized it might not have been the best idea in the world.

The Gull Island Whaling Museum was on Fisher's Path, just before Hagan's Marina. It was housed in an old white clapboard whaling captain's house, complete with a widow's walk on the roof and a gift shop in the former front parlor.

The girls wandered from room to room, reading about the whaling trade, running their hands over an enormous old skiff, *oohing* and *aahing* over intricately carved scrimshaw, and examining old harpoons and whales' teeth.

However, it soon became clear that Kate had a homing device that brought her directly to every picture, painting, or captain's log that described some sort of tragedy at sea. Boats ramming rocks, whales overturning skiffs, mutinies, storms, everything. Twice, Hillary found her standing, slack-jawed, in front of yet another gruesome display, and she had put her arm around Kate's shoulder and gently led her away.

"Katie, you know, we're not going on some long voyage. We're not even going far offshore. And the only whales around these days are busy trying to outswim the whale-watching boats from Newport."

"I think we should tell Gee," Kate had whispered.

"No," Hillary had firmly replied. But inside she was worried that Kate might cave in in a moment of fear and weakness and spill the beans. Even afterward, when Gee took them out to lunch at Cabot's, Hillary watched Kate like a hawk, ready to jump in if she so much as breathed a word about the flag planting.

Back at the house, Hillary was exhausted from her vigilance. While Gee drove off to a Ladies' Village Improvement Society meeting, Hillary called an emergency powwow in her room.

"Guys, we're in the home stretch. The boat's in pretty good shape, we've got the flag ready, we've got most of our supplies lined up, we've got a date, and we're pretty sure we know where we're going. Let's not cave in now and tell Gee, okay?" She looked around at the others to see what they were thinking.

"Obviously," said Neeve.

"I won't," said Phoebe.

But Kate was quiet for a moment. "I guess I won't, but I still think we should, so I guess I'm with you, but under protest."

"Don't be such a baby, Kate," said Neeve crossly. But it came out a little too harshly and Kate started to cry. "Oh, come on!" Neeve protested.

"Don't be mean to Kate, Neeve," said Hillary as she moved to Kate's side and put her arm around her. "She's not trying to wreck things. She's just scared." Kate was usually the one to rush to people's defense, so under the circumstances, Hillary felt she had to do it for her.

"You know what? I'm scared, too," admitted Phoebe as she looked Kate right in the eye. "I'm scared sailing-wise, I'm scared of having a run-in with Sloan even though I hate her, I'm scared of restarting some big feud, and I'm scared that Gee will get mad at us. But you know something else? These guys —" she gestured to Neeve and Hillary "— always get me to do things I'd never do on my own. I finally had to face the fact that these are the kinds of adventures I'd never have, never even think up, by myself. So I think we should just rise above our fears and go along with it, because in the long run, we'll look back on it and laugh, just like our dads."

Hillary beamed at Phoebe. "Thanks, Bee."

"Wow. Who knew Jane Austen had a wild streak?" teased Neeve in a murmur.

Kate had stopped crying. "Okay. I guess." She sniffed and wiped her eyes. "I've been trying to get psyched up, and I finally came up with one thing I could do that would be fun. Do you want to see what I did this morning?"

"Yes!" they agreed.

Kate led them downstairs and out through the drizzle to the boat shed. She flung open the doors with a flourish and said "Ta da!"

On the prow of the boat, she'd painted a vicious shark's mouth, complete with dozens of sharp white teeth, and two blank sharky eyes above it.

The others were shocked at first then collapsed into gales of laughter.

"That is the most un-Martha Stewart thing I've ever seen!" yelled Neeve. "It's brilliant!"

Kate smiled proudly, her eyes still red from the recent tears.

"Totally rad," said Hillary, wrapping Kate in a hug. "Thank you."

"So you're still in?" ventured Phoebe.

"Yeah, I guess," admitted Kate.

The next afternoon, the girls stopped by the hardware store in town to get a new sail before they headed home. Hillary suggested that it was time for a maiden voyage in the *SS Callahan*, if the paint was dry when they got home. A quick sail around the water off Gee's dock, just to get their feet wet, so to speak.

The previous day's rain had stopped, but they were left with a sultry and pervasive humidity that hung heavily in the air and made everything in the house damp. The boat's paint felt sticky, but it didn't come off when they rubbed it, so Hillary declared it ready for immersion.

They hosed down the inside of the boat, leaving it wet but somewhat less icky, and changed into their bathing suits. Hillary grabbed the folded sail from her boat tote in the kitchen and instructed Neeve to get the life jackets from the garage.

"Aye, aye, captain," said Neeve, saluting.

"Bee? Would you please leave a note for Sheila that we went out for a little sail? And Kate, why don't you go grab the flares and stuff up in my room. And maybe a little snack? I'm going to rig up the new sail."

With everyone dispatched to her job, Hillary went back down the yard and set to her task. It wasn't easy and she had a few frustrating moments when she was tempted to just chuck it and wait until Smitty came the next day. He could probably do it with one hand tied behind his back. But she figured they had some momentum going, and she might as well get Kate out there and in the swing of things before her fear grew too large.

As they all reassembled at the boat, Hillary finally clipped the last piece of the sail onto the mast. "There," she said, standing back proudly to admire her handiwork.

"Good job, Hills," said Neeve in admiration.

Hillary retrieved the ancient oars from the boat shed and clipped them onto the gunwales of the boat; then they carried the boat down to the water's edge and piled in. It was cramped, but they all fit. Hillary pushed off from shore. There was a light breeze, and Hillary allowed it to fill the sail and carry them straight out toward Elephant Rock, the first little island off Gee's shore. As they drew near, Neeve suggested they keep going, to the island beyond.

"Um, okay," agreed Hillary. They didn't have the map and she wasn't so familiar with the channel markers around here; she was nervous that she might end up crossing into waters where she wasn't so confident of her abilities. But the last thing she wanted to do was scare Kate, so she pressed on, reluctant to voice any objections.

"Should we make for this island and drop anchor? We could explore it a bit if I can find a good place to put in."

Hillary was uncharacteristically tentative in her suggestions. She didn't want to be too aggressive about sailing today; it was enough of an achievement to have gotten them all on the boat.

"Sure!" said Kate enthusiastically. Hillary smiled. She'd forgotten to factor in that Kate would *always* be happy to get off a boat.

Hillary approached a small sandy beach on the near side of the tiny island, tacking the boat in her struggle to keep the sail filled with air. It was slow going, but the others didn't seem to notice. They reached the beach and Hillary stood slightly to grab the anchor from the small puddle of seawater in the bow of the boat. The boat canted a little to the side as she stood.

"Whoa!" cried Kate, grabbing onto the side of the boat with both hands.

"Sorry." Hillary grinned in embarrassment and sat down heavily with the anchor on her lap. She hadn't wanted to ask anyone else to do the dirty work of grabbing the anchor, so she'd done it herself. She thought of Tucker's emphasis on not standing up in a boat and cringed; what an amateur mistake!

She paid out some of the anchor's rope and then tossed the anchor itself overboard. The water was shallow so it didn't take long for the anchor to hit bottom.

"I think we'll need to wade in a little, so we'd better ditch our shoes," she said.

Phoebe was not pleased at the physical effort required, and Kate was skittish about imagined sharks. But to Hillary's relief, Neeve teased them and jollied them along until they were on shore.

Once on the island, they made a brief tour. It was rocky, with moldy green lichen growing in the cracks of the rocks, and some sea gull droppings. Kate had remembered to bring the snack from the boat; so they sat at the island's highest point, on an enormous granite boulder, and ate a snack in the still, mid-afternoon mugginess.

They discussed the various islands they could see from their vantage point, having friendly arguments about what they thought they remembered from the maps. But then a light fog started to roll in, and Hillary announced that it was time to go. Kate looked nervous, as if she'd forgotten they'd need to get back into the boat to get home.

The girls clambered back down to the shore, put on their life jackets, and waded out to the boat. Back on board, Hillary's stomach clutched uneasily when she looked at the bottom of the boat. What had been a tiny puddle of water was now nearly eight inches of water — the boat was leaking, big time!

The others noticed immediately, and a small panic ensued. Hillary tried to remain calm as the others looked to her for some kind of instructions.

"What do we do, Hillary?" asked Kate urgently.

"Um . . . did anyone see a bailer on board?" Hillary knew there wasn't one, but she couldn't think of anything else to suggest.

"Hillary! You're supposed to be the captain! You're supposed to check for these things!" said Kate. Her fear was making her frantic and accusatory.

Hillary was speechless in her panic.

"Kate, shh. You're not being helpful. Hillary, just make a decision and tell us what to do." Neeve's firmness comforted Hillary.

There was a brief pause as Hillary gathered her wits about her. "Okay. Okay. Kate, the iced tea bottles you brought, from our snack. Get them out and everyone take one and use it to bail. I'm going to try to get us going because we won't take water in as fast if we're moving." She pulled up the anchor and began fiddling with the sail and the tiller. But there was no wind. Luckily, the others were beginning to make progress with the water in the boat; it seemed to be a small, seeping leak in the front, but not a monstrous gash.

"Alright. There's no wind. I'm going to take down the sail and we're going to try to row. Phoebe, hand me those paddles, please." Phoebe did as she was told, and Hillary fitted the paddles into the oarlocks and began to row. The oars were thick and rough, and the water felt like lead as Hillary pulled and pulled. Their progress was minimal.

"It seems like the tide is moving against us, like it's pushing us away from land," said Hillary finally. "I'd say we should wait it out but I'm worried about the leak."

"Here, let me try," said Neeve. She crept over to the middle bench and began to row. Over the next hour, they each took turns at the oars but made very little progress. Their constant bailing kept the water level at a steady three inches.

"What time is it?" asked Kate finally.

Phoebe glanced at her watch. "Five o'clock. We've been out here for a long time. I wonder if Gee's worried," she said.

"Do you think we should send up a flare?" asked Kate nervously.

Hillary was starting to feel hopeless when she felt a tiny puff of air on her cheek. Could the wind be picking up?

Sure enough, over the next fifteen minutes, a breeze slowly built up and the tide began to turn back in. The girls were giddy with relief as Hillary got the boat going, and they all felt triumphant when they pulled into Gee's dock at five-thirty.

As they pulled the boat to shore, the screen door slammed and they saw Gee racing down the lawn. The pink cardigan around her shoulders billowed out behind her like a sail.

"Girls! *Girls!* Where have you been?! I've been beside myself!" She was quickly at their side, half-angry and half-relieved and hugging and inspecting all of them. "You're all exhausted! And what happened to your hands?" She had noticed how gingerly they were using their hands, which were covered in blisters from the rowing. "Good lord, you left that note and didn't say where you were going or when you'd be back! And you've been gone for ages. Oh, I thought I was going to have to call the Coast Guard. Or your parents! Can you imagine?!"

The girls were ashamed and they all apologized to Gee for

their carelessness. They explained what had happened as Gee led them up to the house to do some first aid on their hands.

After everyone was sorted out and had been swabbed, creamed, bandaged, and otherwise refreshed, Gee had them all sit at the kitchen table for a chat. Sheila hovered in the background, nervously wringing her hands.

First, Gee declared that she would arrange to have "a local boatman" pick up the boat early the next morning and fix it immediately. (Hillary swallowed hard. She knew Gee meant Smitty. They'd need the boat back by Saturday afternoon at the latest; that only gave him two days to fix it! She hoped he could do it. She also hoped Sheila could bake the scones in time for his arrival.) Next Gee insisted they create rules and responsibilities for the boat. Hillary noted that they virtually echoed what Tucker had said that day at The Dip.

Kate was in charge of putting together a safety kit and checking it each time they set sail. Phoebe was in charge of checking the tides and weather every time, before they set sail. Neeve was in charge of communications, making sure that Gee or Sheila knew where and when they were going and when they'd be back. And Hillary was in charge of the boat itself, and everyone else, once they were on it. Furthermore, no one was to be out on the water after four PM, no one was to go out alone on the boat, and they had to bring a two-way radio with them whenever they went. Gee told them to pick one up at the hardware store the next day and charge it to her. Finally, Gee took an uncharacteristically stern tone. She told them she expected total compliance with her rules, or the boat would be put off limits for the rest of the summer. The girls nodded solemnly in agreement. They understood.

At this point, they were all limp with exhaustion, so Gee suggested showers or a little nap before dinner, and she said she'd go call the boat man. Hillary had thought that they might be punished, but Gee seemed to think the experience itself had been punishing enough. So the girls trooped upstairs to Kate and Neeve's room and began speaking in whispers.

A moment later there was a knock on the door, and Sheila appeared.

"I'm sorry to barge in on yas, but we need to talk." She perched on the edge of Kate's bed and looked at the girls. "Ya gave me a real fright there, earlier. I'm responsible for yas when yer grandmother's not around, and I felt I'd failed her."

The girls felt terrible. Hillary was first to apologize and the others quickly followed. But Sheila waved away their apologies.

"It's fine, now. Yer all back safe. But I have to insist that ya tell yer grandmother about yer plan. Or I will. I can't risk having anything happen to yas — for yer own sake, yer grandmother's sake, or yer parent's sake. Maybe I'm getting old and it's making me a nervous Nelly, but yer young and inexperienced, too. Ya know, I lost a brother to the sea when he was about yer age, and something like that never leaves ya."

"Oh my gosh, we're so sorry, Sheila!" said Neeve.

"That's horrible," agreed Hillary in a quiet voice.

"Ya, well, I'd just hate to see something like that happen when it can be avoided."

Everyone was silent for a moment, and then Sheila spoke again.

"So will yas do it? Will you tell yer grandmother, for the love of God?"

Everyone looked at Hillary expectantly.

She took a deep breath.

"Yes," she agreed. And she stood to go and find Gee.

CHAPTER SIXTEEN

Confession

*H*illary could hear Gee talking on the phone in her room. She must've been telling someone about what had just happened because she could hear Gee saying "It gave me such a fright!" Hillary felt guilty. She knocked gently on Gee's door.

"Come in!" called Gee.

Hillary pushed the door open and saw Gee sitting at her skirted dressing table, the phone pressed to her ear. Gee smiled and winked at Hillary then motioned her in to sit on the low, pink loveseat.

"Yes, yes. *Quite!*" Gee was saying. "Excuse me, though, Smitty. I'm going to have to run. I've just got one of the culprits here in my room. . . . Yes. Tomorrow. Seven-thirty. We'll see you then." Gee replaced the phone in its cradle and turned to Hillary.

Good, Smitty's coming, thought Hillary. *That's one good thing.*

"Well," Gee sighed. "What an adventurous day you've had, my dear."

Hillary sighed, too. "I am so sorry, Gee. It's really all my fault. The others . . . they were just going along with me. I was the irresponsible one."

"Oh, my dear Hillary, I'm not angry. I understand all too well how youngsters can get swept away by an exciting idea and just throw caution to the wind, if you'll excuse the pun. I just thank the Lord everything turned out alright."

Hillary paused, grateful to have such an understanding grandmother. Then she took a deep breath. "Gee, what I meant to say is, well . . . what I'm trying to tell you . . ."

Gee looked at her expectantly.

Hillary gulped and looked away. "We want to plant the flag." There. She'd said it. She glanced back at Gee for her reaction.

Gee rolled her eyes up in exasperation, then sighed heavily, looking down at her hands, which lay folded in her lap. Then she looked back sharply at Hillary. "Why?" she asked.

Hillary couldn't tell if Gee was mad or not, but she decided to press on, get it all out in the open and let the cards fall where they might.

"It's something I've been thinking about for a long time; ever since I knew I was coming here for the summer. I'm not trying to make trouble or anything. . . . I mean, I don't want to stir up a lot of bad memories or get anyone mad at anyone else. It's more sort of . . . a selfish thing, I guess." Hillary paused to gauge Gee's reaction.

"Go on," said Gee quietly.

"It's just . . . I feel so disconnected from my dad, and . . ." Hillary's voice suddenly caught. Darn it! She hated tears. She wouldn't be a crybaby! She took a deep breath and started again. "And I just felt like, if we did it, it would make him proud of me. And maybe bring us closer, you know, since we're not together that much anymore. I just thought it was, like, a real Callahan thing to do. You know, since my dad and everyone used to do it when they were growing up."

Gee quickly rose from the little pink tufted stool where she was sitting and stepped over to the loveseat. She sat and put her arms around Hillary and gave her an enormous hug. The tears Hillary had been fighting began to leak from the corners of her eyes and she pulled herself from Gee to impatiently brush them away. "Sorry," she mumbled.

"Don't be silly. I don't mind if you cry. After the year you've had, I'd say you deserve to shed more than a few tears. Here." She plucked a pretty pink-and-white handkerchief from her dressing table drawer and handed it to Hillary. Hillary mopped her eyes and sniffed, regaining control of herself.

Gee bit her lip, lost in thought for a moment.

Hillary continued. "Anyway, we don't *have* to do it. I mean, I don't want to cause any big problems for you or anything. You know, start up bad things with the Bickets again. I had just thought it would be fun and sort of silly, but Sheila seems to think it's a terrible, dangerous thing for us to do . . ."

Gee smiled suddenly. "Well of course she would," she said.

"Why?" Hillary was confused.

"Well obviously, because . . ." Gee caught herself in what she was about to say. She was confused now. "Wait, Sheila didn't tell you . . . ?" Gee paused.

"You mean that her brother died at sea when he was our age?" asked Hillary.

"Um . . . yes, yes of course." Gee seemed to be hiding something suddenly. *This is turning into a strange conversation,* thought Hillary.

"Is that it?" pressed Hillary. She searched Gee's clear blue eyes for more information, but Gee had recovered. She had nothing else to reveal.

"Yes," said Gee firmly. "That's why. Now. I must tell you my feelings about the flag planting. I have always thought that it was a childish game. Not dangerous, just . . . a little tacky, if you want to know the truth. I didn't like it when the boys used to do it because I felt it implied some sort of rich kid, spoiled brat ownership of Gull Island. The whole, 'We were here first' business that I can't stand about New England." She peered at Hillary. "Do you understand what I mean?"

"Um, sort of. But what's the New England part?"

"Oh, just the way that some people — particularly in Boston and Newport — are so obsessed with the early arrival of their families in New England, back in the 1700s or even 1600s. And they think that anyone whose family came later — you know, like immigrants, especially the Irish who came in the 1800s — are inferior to them. Newcomers, and thus unworthy of equal status or treatment. It's a load of hooey! Americans are Americans whether their families got here four hundred years ago or yesterday!"

Hillary nodded in agreement and Gee continued.

"As for it being a Callahan tradition, or proving yourself as a Callahan, that's just silliness. You are now and always will be a part of this family, no matter what. The only true 'Callahan' traits, as I like to think of them, are generosity, enthusiasm, good sportsmanship, manners, and a sense of humor; and you've got all of those in spades. Planting a silly old flag couldn't possibly improve you in that department."

Hillary nodded again. "Thanks," she whispered.

"Now. I don't know if you've had much contact with the Bickets, but they can be an ornery lot; not all of them, mind you." Gee laughed suddenly. "Lord knows there are good Bickets! But for myself, and my dealings with them, I don't actually mind if you do it. We've pretty much made our peace over the last few years, and I know that something as small as this won't undo all of that. But I'd hate to see you getting wrapped up in any ill will or revenge kinds of things with the difficult ones. It can be a tricky business, dealing with them."

"Yeah, I know," said Hillary drily. Now she rolled her eyes and Gee laughed.

"But really, I think I'm mostly worried about you, that you think you need to prove something to your father or somehow earn his admiration. You must know that your father is over the moon about you. He's so proud of you and he thinks the sun rises and sets on you, as of course he should! He's beside himself about the divorce and mainly because he can't stand being separated from you. He'd die if he knew he'd somehow put you in a position where you'd do something risky just to please him. Do you understand that? He adores you, just the way you are."

Hillary nodded. She didn't trust her voice to speak.

Gee sighed. "However, I know that part of growing up is doing things on your own, learning from trial and error, having adventures . . . and Gull is a wonderful place for all of that." She paused. "I can't believe I'm about to say this, but it's only because I trust you completely; you are a mature and capable young woman and I'd feel safe on any boat you were captaining. So here it is: If you feel that the flag-planting is something that you must do, then you have my blessing. I think that your reasons for doing it are legitimate, to you, and that so far, you've approached it in the right way, excepting, of course, the little misadventure of this afternoon." Gee winked and Hillary felt a cautious smile lifting the corners of her mouth.

"I will have a talk with Sheila about it and put her mind at ease. We will have my friend Smitty fix the boat so that we don't have to worry about that anymore. Now, do you know where you're going? And when? Do you know the waters? How to go about it? I'm not sure where you are in this process."

So Hillary related all the progress they'd made, and Gee laughed here and there in surprise. "You see! I knew you were capable! Goodness, to think all this has been going on right under my nose! I'm ashamed of my ignorance! But then, twelve-year-olds can be the sneakiest creatures on Earth! Of course I knew all about the boat repairs, but I thought that was just a fun project. And Nelly Merrihew told me you'd been in and looking at maps and things, and Truman St. John mentioned he was looking for something for the lot of you. And then when I saw Smitty at church last week he said you'd been by, but I just never put it all together. I was just glad you were out meeting all the locals!"

Hillary grinned. "It sure is a small island."

"Yes it is," agreed Gee. And then they got down to details.

First, and most important, they agreed that there would only be one planting of the flag, because Gee didn't want it to turn into a summer-long battle with the Bickets again. They agreed that the girls would review their route to the island with Tucker, just so they'd know where to go and how. They agreed that the girls could go the coming week, in order to accomplish the task before their fathers arrived. And Gee said she would speak to Sheila about the situation and let her know that the girls had her reluctant approval for the endeavor.

The relief of having everything out in the open washed over Hillary like a cool breeze. Even her limbs felt lighter for having shared the secret. Because, to be totally honest with herself, she had to admit she'd started to feel bad about keeping their plans from Gee. It felt right to have finally confessed, and even better to have received Gee's blessing, of sorts.

As they were wrapping everything up, Hillary began to feel concern for the others, waiting back in the bedroom for word from her. They probably figured Gee was chewing Hillary out, and they all must've felt terrible by now. Hillary asked Gee to come with her to explain everything to the others, and Gee agreed.

As they rose to go down the hall, Gee stopped and hugged Hillary once more. "You mustn't ever feel like you're not a Callahan, my dear. No matter what happens with your parents, you are always going to be one of us, and that's not something you need to prove."

"Thanks, Gee," said Hillary into Gee's shoulder. "Thanks for everything."

They all had to admit that telling Gee was a good idea in the end. They hadn't realized how nerve-wracking it was, trying to keep the secret from her. And now, with Smitty coming in the morning, and everything else sorted out, there wasn't much for the girls to do, flag-planting-wise. So they showered and changed and ambled down to the kitchen to se if dinner would be ready soon.

Sheila was subdued. She was clearly relieved that Hillary had told Gee about the flag planting, but she didn't seem happy that Gee had okayed it.

"If the missus says it's fine, then it's alright with me," she shrugged.

Hillary suddenly felt bad that it hadn't worked out how Sheila had hoped. She wondered what Gee had been about to say about Sheila during their conversation earlier. Because there had definitely been something, and then Gee had changed her mind. Strange. She'd have to tell the others and see what they thought.

After dinner, while the others played *Trivial Pursuit,* Hillary lay on the couch and watched television, mulling over her earlier conversation with Gee. Other than the flag-planting specifics, she hadn't had time yet to think about what Gee had said to her. She definitely appreciated all the nice things Gee had said — especially the stuff about her dad already being proud of her, and her not needing to prove she was a Callahan. But she wasn't sure she quite believed Gee. If she could just get this flag planted, then she'd feel alright. She knew it. Hillary gave a huge yawn. And they were so close now. Just a few minor details to sort out. Her eyes drooped sleepily and she nestled herself deeper into the couch.

But suddenly, her eyelids snapped up like window shades and her heart dropped like an anchor. She'd just realized that everything that stood between her and a planted flag depended on someone else. The boat from Smitty, the map from Talbot's dad, the route from Tucker, the flag from Kate. It was all out of Hillary's control. And Hillary did not like that feeling one bit.

CHAPTER SEVENTEEN

Ups and Downs

To Hillary's relief, Smitty turned out to be a man of his word. At seven-thirty the next morning, his ancient pickup truck rattled and crunched its way up Gee's long driveway, with a rickety boat trailer swaying precariously behind it. Based on Sloan's nasty comments that day at the dock, Hillary was at least expecting Smitty to be late. But sure enough, the girls hadn't even left for clinic yet, and there he was: knocking on the screen door, dressed in blue overalls, a grubby white t-shirt, and a bandanna, tied hippie-style on his head.

Everyone grinned when they saw him, and Sheila went to let him in. Once inside, he grabbed Sheila in a big hug and wheeled her around in a circle. The girls exchanged stunned glances. Was he her boyfriend? But no, Sheila was brusque as ever, patting her hair back into place and smoothing out her shapeless housedress, glancing self-consciously over her shoulder at the girls. No, it wasn't anything romantic, that was clear. But Hillary noted there was a tiny mischievous sparkle in Sheila's eye that she'd never seen before. Smitty had put it there.

"Well if it isn't the Mormon Tabernacle Choir!" exclaimed Smitty on seeing the cousins gathered around the breakfast table. He put his hands on his hips and pretended to scrutinize them. "Butter wouldn't melt in your mouths!" he concluded at last.

"Hi, Smitty," they said shyly. They knew that he knew all about their misadventure of the previous day.

Sheila was all business again, bustling around the counter, packing up Smitty's scones in a pastry tin. "Girls, why don't one of yas tell Mrs. Callahan that Smitty's here?" Gee was upstairs, still showering after her swim. Hillary went to get her.

"And why don't one of *yas* show me where this old stinkpot of yours is?" Smitty winked at his imitation of Sheila, but the girls were confused. Stinkpot?

"The boat, the vessel, the *SS Callahan* . . . ?"

Everyone giggled, and Neeve rose to show him.

Later, as they cycled to clinic, Hillary prayed that Smitty would prove Sloan wrong again and return their boat quickly. By Tuesday, at the latest, as he'd promised. They'd be sure to have the map by then, and they could meet with Tucker Wednesday, and still be able to plant the flag on Thursday afternoon, before their dads arrived Friday. A week from today.

But as Hillary had watched Smitty's pickup rattle back down the driveway with their boat grinning away sharkishly on the trailer, it scared her anew to think it was all in Smitty's hands for now. Because, after all, he was a Bicket.

The four cousins returned that afternoon from a hazy, hot day at clinic and Macaroni Beach, to find a message from Talbot. He told Sheila to tell them that he had "the stuff they needed" and to meet him at The Dip that night at eight-thirty. The girls were elated and high-fived and whooped their way to the fridge for a celebratory snack.

At precisely eight-twenty-nine, the four girls marched into The Dip. Gee had driven them and had volunteered to wait in the car with a new magazine while the girls went to meet Talbot; she'd sensed from their demeanor that they didn't want "an old-lady chaperone" (as she'd put it) to accompany them. The girls had dressed up for the occasion, and Neeve had produced her seemingly bottomless makeup kit and embellished everyone, "just a wee bit." Gee had taken one look at them and rolled her eyes heavenward, but she hadn't made them take it off.

The place was packed with kids and families, but they quickly spotted Talbot seated at the counter with a black-and-white Awful-Awful in front of him (Oreo ice cream with hot fudge and marshmallow topping). He waved in greeting and the girls made their way through the crowded room to join him. Lying on the floor below his feet was a small shopping bag with a large book of dogeared sea charts sticking out the top. Phoebe shamelessly peered over Talbot's knees until he finally got the hint and reached down to lift the bag up to the counter.

"But, hey, check this, there's something wack about this book that you're gonna be interested in," said Talbot, reaching into the bag.

"What?" asked Phoebe, always interested in book stuff.

"I think it's the Bickets'!"

"No way!" said Neeve excitedly. "Bust it out! Let's have a look!"

Talbot pulled the wire-bound book from the bag. Its pages were ragged and thick with dried sea spray. Across the front cover, in block letters, it said BICKET. Phoebe lunged to cover the word, looking over her shoulder for spies. The others laughed.

"Why would your dad have that?" asked Kate.

"Oh, because he bought his boat from Sloan's dad. It was Sloan's grandfather's trawler, and then when he died, Mr. Bicket, Sloan's dad, just wanted to get rid of it. So Mr. Bicket had Smitty sell it to my dad for a really low price so that he didn't have to clean it out himself. The grandfather was this old, Irish fisherman guy. Lots of junk on board, you know? It was like Sloan's dad was kind of ashamed of him."

He thumbed his way toward the back of the book until he reached the page he was looking for. "Check it out!" he said proudly.

Phoebe took the book from his hands, and the others bunched together to peer over his shoulders. She furrowed her brow in concentration and scanned the two-page spread. Sure enough, just where she expected to find it, there was a tiny, perfectly gull-shaped island, clearly marked "Quocasset. Little Gull Island." On this map, the island's shape was much clearer and more definite than on the more recent map Mrs. Merrihew had found for them at the library, and for this the girls were thankful. Now they had no doubt about where they were heading.

"Yes!" said Hillary, pumping her fist. "That's it!"

"Hey guys," a voice said behind them. It was Tucker!

And Sloan.

Phoebe slammed the book shut and hugged it to her chest, hiding the name on the cover.

"Hi," the Callahans replied to Tucker. Sloan and the girls eyed each other warily, then Sloan looked away, pretending to be bored by them.

"What's that you've got there?" asked Tucker curiously.

"Nothing," said Phoebe. Sloan turned back to look carefully at what Phoebe was holding. She narrowed her eyes and then seemed to think for a second, and finally she spoke.

"Wasn't that your grandmother I saw out there, waiting for you?" she said, in a condescending voice.

The girls were taken aback. How was Sloan able to make something so innocent sound so babyish and wrong? Like they were losers because their grandmother had brought them out that night.

"Yeah," said Neeve defiantly. "We don't have a live-in babysitter." She stared pointedly at Tucker. Sloan turned red and so did Tucker.

But before Sloan could think of another insult, a stool opened at the counter two spots down and Sloan quickly pounced on it. "Tucky!" she whined, when he didn't follow her immediately.

"Coming," he called back.

Hillary had to seize the moment. "Hey, Tucker, one quick thing. Can you come over this week, like maybe Wednesday, to go over our route to the island with us? Gee said she'd feel more comfortable with our going if you had approved the plan."

Tucker was pleased by the compliment. He smiled. "Sure. But do me a favor and don't let Sloan know, okay? I just can't deal with any more of her nagging or interference. She's driving me crazy with her whole obsession with you guys."

Hillary's mind flashed briefly to clinic, where Sloan continued to steal glances at them that were really, blatantly envious. She still wasn't sure what to make of it.

"Sorry about the babysitter comment, Tucker. It was just the first thing that came to my mind," said Neeve quietly.

"That's alright," said Tucker, and he smiled a lopsided smile and slipped away.

"So! An encounter with the enemy!" laughed Talbot. The

cousins smiled halfheartedly. It was too true to really be funny.

Suddenly they could hear Sloan's snotty voice floating down the counter in their direction. "Yes, and Tucker's taking me to this little island my family owns for a picnic this week. It's called Little Gull Island. . . ."

The girls looked at each other in alarm. Her family *owns*? Tucker's taking her?

They craned their heads to see who she was speaking to, and it was Lark, the pretty Asian girl from clinic. Lark was nodding enthusiastically at Sloan's plans, but behind Sloan's back, Tucker was rolling his eyes at the Callahans and shaking his head.

"What do you think that means?" asked Neeve, narrowing her eyes. "He's not taking her or they don't own it?"

"I don't think anyone can own those little islands," suggested Talbot hopefully. "But it might not be a bad idea to double-check."

"Aaargh. That's all we need!" said Hillary in frustration.

Kate glanced at her watch. "If we're going to get ice cream . . . ," she began.

"Yeah, we should get a move on," agreed Hillary. "What did Gee want again?"

They ordered their ice cream and thanked Talbot for all of his help. Then Neeve spontaneously invited him to the family cookout the following Saturday night. The others were surprised, but Talbot was so pleased that they immediately saw what a great idea it had been to invite him.

"So, yo, good luck if I don't see you before Saturday, okay? And call me if you need anything else," said Talbot.

"Thanks, Talbot." They all waved. And with their paper-wrapped cones and a coffee ice cream with hot fudge sauce for Gee, they scrambled to the car to grill Gee about the ownership of the little islands off Gull.

CHAPTER EIGHTEEN

Timing

The next few days were cold and rainy, that kind of unpredictable late June weather that appears in New England and reminds people why settlers named it New *England*. Hillary kept finding herself at the windows of Gee's house, staring out as the rain pelted the pool and the little islands in the sound, beyond. Gee hadn't known anything about the Bickets owning Little Gull Island, and, although she'd made a few calls, she hadn't been able to find anything out for sure. The town assessor was looking into it for her, but there hadn't been any progress.

Clinic was canceled on Monday and Tuesday, due to the bad weather, and Gee worked hard to keep the girls occupied and their spirits up. She sent them bowling on Sunday, and took them to a matinee on Monday afternoon. They played board games and baked muffins and did jigsaw puzzles. Gee even let Neeve give her a makeover, and the result was so hilarious that Gee had laughed until her eyes teared, causing the three coats of mascara to run down her cheeks like muddy rivers. "I look like a Dallas Cowboys Cheerleader!" she'd cried.

During a brief break in the rain showers, the girls had ridden their bikes to the Little Store, just to shake off some of their cabin fever. Hillary had asked Farren whether or not it was possible that someone could own Little Gull Island. Farren hadn't been sure, but she'd placed a call to the county clerk on the mainland and he'd said he would look into it and get right back to her. That had been Monday morning. Since then, they had had no word from Smitty, no word from the county clerk or town assessor, and there was no hope of getting out on the water because of the weather.

Now, Tuesday afternoon, charcoal gray storm clouds still blanketed the island. The tops of the trees swayed in the gusty wind, and there were whitecaps on the sound. Puddles formed around the yard, and Phoebe and Hillary's bedroom had just nearly flooded because Phoebe had cracked a window for some fresh air while she read in her bed.

Hillary lay restlessly on her own bed, staring at the ceiling. She was antsy from being indoors for so long, and she was beginning to feel that their flag planting was a lost cause. Her optimism and enthusiasm for the project were now congealing into dismay and regret. All she had hoped to accomplish this summer was to plant that flag. But if they didn't have it done before their dads came, there was really no point. For the hundredth time, she pictured herself taking her dad out to the island and showing him, pointing to the flag and saying "I did that. I am a Callahan, just like you. Forever." And her dad would smile, and hug her, and . . . what? Promise to come back to them? Hillary shook her head and heaved herself onto her side. In the darkest of moments, she had to ask herself: What did she really think would happen anyway? Because the flag planting wouldn't bring him back. Nothing really could. Nothing she could do, anyway.

In the distance, Hillary heard the phone ring, but she didn't think anything of it. The phone rang constantly at Gee's house. But soon, she heard footsteps coming up the stairs, and there was a light tap on their door.

"Girls?" Gee whispered. She thought they might be sleeping.

"Yes?" replied Hillary. She and Phoebe both sat up in their beds. "Come in!"

The door squeaked open and Gee's head popped in. "I have good news!"

"What?!" Hillary was suddenly energized.

"Farren called. The Bickets do not own Little Gull Island. It's part of the National Seashore preserve. No one can own it! Isn't that wonderful?"

"Whoo-hoo!" Hillary jumped up on her bed and began bouncing. "Yee haw!"

Her shouts drew Neeve and Kate from across the hall, and Gee happily repeated the news.

"Now I have some not-so-good news," said Gee, sobering. "Smitty called while I was on the other line. Due to the horrid weather, he won't have the boat back to us until Friday."

"Nooooo!" moaned Hillary. She sank back down onto her bed. "That's too late!"

"Are you sure?" asked Gee anxiously. "Couldn't you go out Friday morning, if he gets it here in time . . . ?"

"But we have clinic . . . ," protested Hillary.

Gee's eyes twinkled for a moment. "I think that under the circumstances, you could miss clinic on Friday."

"Really? You mean it? Oh, Gee, that is so great! Thank you!" Hillary hopped off her bed and gave Gee a huge hug. It would be right down to the wire, but they could do it. They had to.

The sun finally returned to Gull Island on Wednesday. Hillary could hardly believe her eyes when she awoke that day to see the rays streaming through the light cotton curtains on the windows. She sprang out of bed and dashed to the window and let out a cry of joy when she saw the cloudless, blue sky above. The weather had finally given them a reprieve.

"It could rain for the rest of the summer — except Friday, of course — and I wouldn't care!" declared Hillary. Phoebe just groaned and put her head under the covers.

But in fact, everyone was happy and raring to go that morning. Clinic passed quickly and the girls were eagerly awaiting

Tucker when he arrived at Gee's house at three o'clock to review their proposed route to Little Gull.

They set up out by the pool, laying the maps all around the glass-topped table. Phoebe had the notebook, in which she'd noted Friday's high and low tide times from the chalkboard at Hagan's Marina, and a pen, which they would use to trace their route along the up-to-date chart from the library.

Consulting the old chart that Talbot had given the girls, Tucker reviewed the previous notations he'd made on the new chart and made a few small alterations. The girls watched carefully as he talked about areas to avoid, and markers to keep in sight. Then he double-checked the tidal tables and had Phoebe confirm the high and low tide times. At the end, when they all agreed that they understood what to do, Tucker reminded them of the full moon and the spring tide once again.

"You really need to set sail just as the tide is going out, and come back when the tide is coming in. It's not that I expect anything dangerous to happen, it's just that you could easily get stuck on your way out to the island if you don't set sail when you're supposed to — the water will be so shallow in some places that you could run aground."

"So what time should we leave by?" asked Phoebe, her brow furrowed in concentration as she made notations in the notebook.

"I'd say by seven-thirty. Eight at the latest," said Tucker.

"And what about coming back?" asked Phoebe, looking up at him.

"Well, high tide is at three o'clock. With these narrow channels through here that you need to take, the water will rise quickly and be moving fast when the tide is at its highest. I'd say you should leave there by two o'clock, so you don't have to navigate through any tricky, rushing water. And whatever you do, don't try to go against the tide when it's on its way in. You could end up stuck, or worse."

"What's worse?" whimpered Kate.

"Capsized," said Tucker grimly. "But honestly, don't worry. If you stick to your schedule and follow your plan, you'll be absolutely fine."

Sheila came outside then, with a tray of warm, fresh chocolate chip cookies and a pitcher of cold milk. She liked Tucker, the girls had noted, and his involvement in the flag-planting plans seemed to make her feel better about the whole thing.

"So that's yer route, then?" she asked, leaning over the table to look at the map.

"Uh-huh," said Hillary through a mouthful of cookie.

"Looks good," said Sheila. "Never thought I'd say it, but I'm impressed by yas. You've really worked hard on this and I wish yas the best of luck."

Hillary was touched, and she could tell that the others were, too.

"Thanks, Sheila," said Kate. "That means a lot."

"In fact, I think I have a thing or two I might dig up fer the journey. I'm going to take meself up fer a good look around. Now where did I put those . . ." Sheila walked purposefully back into the house, tapping her upper lip as if trying to jog her memory. The girls giggled.

"Wow! Talk about a change of heart!" said Phoebe.

"I think she's in love with Tucker, so whatever he thinks is okay is okay with her," said Neeve boldly.

Tucker blushed. "Aw, come on!"

This made the girls laugh harder.

"I think this is my cue to leave, so you can all have a good girly giggle at my expense," said Tucker with a smile, as he picked up his knapsack and stuffed his feet back into his top-siders. But his face clouded over for a moment and he looked back up at the girls sitting around the table.

"Guys, I do have something to tell you, though. And I've been putting it off because I don't want to upset you."

"Yes?" said Neeve, drawing out the word like a detective on TV.

"Uh, you know how I'm living with the Bickets and all, and I'm sort of privy to, um, inside information . . . ," Tucker stammered.

"What does 'privy' mean?" Kate whispered to Phoebe.

"Like, um, privileged. He's in the know," Phoebe whispered back.

"Well, Sloan's boat is fixed and she's definitely going out to plant that flag of hers."

There was a stunned silence.

Hilary gulped. "When?" she whispered.

"Friday," said Tucker.

CHAPTER NINETEEN

Family Heirlooms

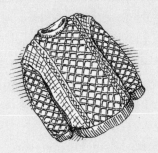

$\mathcal{T}$hursday afternoon, the girls were in Neeve and Kate's room, laying out their supplies for the next day's voyage.

"I still can't believe that traitor!" Neeve was ranting about Smitty finishing Sloan's boat repairs before theirs. She was also planning her outfit for the "expedition," as she called it, and was knee-deep in rejected clothes.

"Neeve, we've been over this. It's not his fault," Kate protested. "You have to put yourself in Smitty's shoes. They're his family. And his best customers. He has to be nice to them. And you have to admit that Sloan had her boat there before us."

"Still," Neeve huffed, examining an embroidered Tibetan vest.

"Look, it's just one more thing we don't need to waste our energy worrying about." Hillary had all but put on blinders, now that she was in full-steam-ahead mode; nothing would stop her at this point. "We can't worry about her or be looking over our shoulder the whole time. We've got to pay attention to what *we're* doing."

Phoebe had her head in the notebook, where she was double-checking their gear list. "Okay, we've got the radio, and it's working . . ."

"Ten-four, good buddy," said Hillary into the mouth-piece. The receiver was on Neeve's bed and it squawked right next to Kate's ear because she was sitting on the braided cotton rug.

"Hillary!" she shouted, clutching her ear.

Hillary grinned. "It works!"

They went through the rest of their supply list while Kate struggled to staple their flag to an old wooden dowel they'd found in the garage. Everything was in order, and the only things left to do were pull out the life vests and oars, and then load the boat.

"As soon as Smitty gets here tomorrow morning, we're leaving," sang Hillary in satisfaction.

"If he gets here!" sniffed Neeve, as she pulled on a pair of zebra-print leggings.

"There!" said Kate. The flag was finished.

There was a knock on the door and Sheila came in with a big duffel bag. "I knew I'd stashed these somewheres safe," she said. She swung the bag into the middle of the room and dropped it on the rug. Then she unzipped it and a powerful moth ball odor wafted over them. The girls gathered around her, peering curiously into the bag. Sheila reached her hand in and pulled out . . . one Irish sweater, two, three, four, five.

"Hey! Zigzags and honeycombs! Those are the Callahan pattern!" said Phoebe. "I remember from when you told us and I wrote it in our notebook."

Kate reached out to take one from Sheila. She fingered the oatmeal-colored, hand-knit wool in its intricate patterns. "Wow. These are beautiful."

"They belonged to yer dads, and yer Uncle Lou. I thought ya'd might like to wear 'em out on yer journey." Sheila sat back on her heels and put her hands on her lap.

"Thanks, Sheila!" they said gratefully. They knew it couldn't have been easy for her to make such a gesture, seeing as how she was against the whole flag-planting plan.

"Well, like I said. I wish yas luck. Yer a good group a' kids and I hope it all turns out fer yas." Sheila stood and dusted her hands off on her skirt. "Now, ya might want to put these outside to air a little before ya put 'em on." Then she left the girls alone to finish up their organizing.

Neeve had fished all the sweaters out of the bag and was shaking them out to see how big they were. Suddenly a piece of white fabric fluttered to the floor.

"What was that?" asked Kate.

"Hmm?" Neeve hadn't noticed it, so Kate scrambled across the rug and picked it up. She unfolded it and shook it, then gasped.

"Guys! Look!" she yelped.

It was the flag. The Callahan family flag — a little tattered and a lot faded, but the name was still clearly there, in green paint, with a little green shamrock — the Irish symbol of good luck — painted right beneath it.

"Leave it to boys to make such a crummy flag," laughed Neeve.

"But what should we do with it, now that we have our own flag?" asked Kate.

Hillary reached for the flag and Neeve handed it to her.

"Staple it to ours," said Phoebe decisively.

"Yes," agreed Hillary quietly, nodding her head as she turned the fabric slowly in her hands.

That night, Hillary couldn't sleep. She was excited, and nervous, and . . . almost sad. Sad that the quest to plant the flag was almost over, or sad that it wasn't making her feel as proud as she would've thought . . . she wasn't sure.

She got up quietly from her bed and crept downstairs to Gee's library, where she turned on a small lamp and grabbed a fluffy, white chenille blanket to toss on the armchair she wanted to sit in. Then she crossed the room to the wall of bookshelves and spied what she had really come for. The thirty identical caramel-colored leather photo albums — documenting year after year of the Callahan family — that she'd been aching to get her hands on for days.

Hillary pulled the first two from the shelf; they were heavy and the leather felt cool and cushiony in her hand. She went back to her armchair, snuggled under the blanket, and began to flip the pages. Gee and Pops on their honeymoon. Gee and Pops standing in front of their first apartment on Beacon Street in Boston. Gee and Pops and their first child — Uncle Bill, Neeve's dad — as a tiny, swaddled infant. Hillary thought about her grandparents' marriage. *What makes people stay married for so long?* she wondered. *Maybe it was all those kids. Maybe my parents should have had more kids.*

She flipped through the first two albums rather quickly, and rose to trade them in for two more. And then two more. They were all filled with cute or funny photos, but somehow, until her dad was old enough to actually look like himself in the pictures, Hillary found them a little too distant to be very interesting. It was like she couldn't connect the knobby-kneed five-year-old called Frankie with her dad, Francis, the way he looked now.

She paused to think back on Gee's words the other day — about being a Callahan. Mentally, she ticked off the list that she'd committed to memory. Generosity. Enthusiasm. Good sportsmanship. Manners. A sense of humor. A tiny corner of her brain called out to her: *"The flag-planting plan goes against all of those traits!"* But she couldn't listen. She'd come too far. She was too close to success to stop now.

She pulled two albums from the other end of the row, and found enough satisfaction within to linger over them. There were pictures of aunts' and uncles' weddings, the christenings and toddlerhoods of her older cousins, family picnics on Macaroni Beach. Everyone was dressed in a sort of funny way to Hillary, even though the pictures were only about twenty years old. She flipped a page and then she stopped.

In the middle of the page was a slightly oversized photo of her parents at a dressy summer dinner. They were seated at a table, very close together, and her dad had his arm around the back of her mom's chair. Her dad must've just said something funny, because he was smiling and her mom's head was thrown back in laughter. Her hand was on his chest. They were clearly in love.

Looking at the picture, Hillary wasn't sure whether to laugh or cry. She was suddenly thrilled and relieved to have proof that her parents had once been so happy together, but at the same time she was sadder than ever that they were no longer happy. She flipped ahead a few pages and found a photo of the whole family that must've been taken at Pops' birthday picnic the year before she was born. All of the aunts and uncles and their spouses were there, and many of the older cousins. Hillary's mom and dad were standing together in the middle; two of Hillary's aunts were laughing at something her mother had said, and one of the uncles standing beside her mom must've been playfully tickling her, because she was laughing and kind of hunched to the side. Hillary smiled. Her mom had fit in really well with her dad's family. She'd always known that.

Hillary sighed and set aside that album. She hefted the last one onto her lap and began slowly flicking through the pages. Here were where the photos of her began. Bent over, looking for shells in the tide pools. Her dad pulling her around Gee's pool as she learned how to swim — huge smiles of pride on his face and hers. A gaggle of cousins at a barbecue, with Hillary sitting on her cousin Chap's lap. Hillary and Neeve in tiny bikini bottoms and little stick-out tummies, holding hands with Gee at the beach.

Gee had been so good to them, always. And this summer more than ever. *Imagine her helping us with the flag planting!* thought Hillary suddenly. *That's pretty darn cool for a grandmother!*

Suddenly, there was a little drumming sound on the door and Hillary jumped. She turned to see Gee, wrapped in her bathrobe, wiggling her fingers hello at Hillary.

"May I?" asked Gee, gesturing at the chair next to Hillary's.

Hillary grinned at the formality. "But of course," she answered in kind.

"Shouldn't you be sound asleep upstairs, storing up energy for the big day?" asked Gee as she crossed the room and sank gracefully into the chair.

"Yeah, totally. I just couldn't sleep," admitted Hillary ruefully.

"What are you looking at?" asked Gee, squinting as she peered at the book in Hillary's lap. Gee was hopeless without her reading glasses.

Hillary closed the book. "Just some old photo albums." She

rubbed the smooth cover and tried to make a joke of it. "You know, studying up on all the names and faces before everyone arrives tomorrow."

Gee reached out and patted Hillary's hand. "Are you okay?" she asked, ignoring Hillary's attempt at humor.

Hillary sighed and leaned her head back against her seat. "You know what? I am. I've been wanting to look at these pictures ever since I saw the albums, but I was scared to. I was worried they'd make me upset all over again, about my parents. But it's weird . . ." She paused. "I was so convinced that I was out of it when I got here. That I wasn't enough of a Callahan, and that I had to prove all this stuff to the family, and to my dad. But, just looking at these albums . . . I'm in them as much as anyone else. And I'm doing all the same stuff, and I look like everyone else, and my dad does. And everyone seemed to like my mom . . . ," she trailed off.

"We still do, my dear. We love her. And we'll always love her," said Gee. "Just like we'll always love you. You'll both be Callahans forever, whether you like it or not!" Gee's eyes twinkled.

"Thanks," Hillary bit her lip to keep her eyes from welling up.

"You know, just the other day, your mother was telling me about what a great year you'd had on the track team, and she was so funny in describing the other kids on the team, and what the meets are like. I'm telling you, she got me crying laughing, just like she always does." Gee laughed, just thinking of it, and shook her head.

Hillary frowned. "What do you mean, just the other day? You talked to my mother?" She herself had been phoning home to check in every few days or so, but her mom hadn't mentioned talking to Gee.

"Well, of course. I could hardly have you here and not speak to her. We check in regularly. I thought you knew that." Gee was surprised.

Hillary shook her head and frowned. "No. I assumed you two would probably never speak again, after the divorce."

Gee was shocked. "Why, Hillary! That's preposterous! I adore your mother. Not just because she was a loving wife to my son for nearly twenty years, and not just because she's the mother of my grandchild. She's a very dear friend, and she always will be, no matter what happens with your parents' marriage."

Hillary wiggled in happiness and drew the blanket more closely around herself. She couldn't believe it, and yet she could. She didn't know what to say, but she felt awash in gratitude to Gee, and to her mom, for being such good people.

"Now what do you think about a dram of warm milk for the two of us? That should get us on the right track to drowsiness, hmm?" said Gee, reaching over to smooth Hillary's hair away from her face.

"Okay." Gee stood to go into the kitchen.

"Gee?" said Hillary. Gee turned back. "Thanks." And she smiled and went out the door.

Five minutes later, when Gee returned with two steaming mugs of milk, Hillary was fast asleep in her chair.

CHAPTER TWENTY

Smooth Sailing

*H*illary slept soundly after all. But she bolted wide awake at six, as the sun was beginning to lighten the sky, and slid out of her bed and down to the kitchen. Sheila was already up, bustling around the kitchen and packing a scrumptious picnic for the girls. Gee sat at the table, her thick, white, terry cloth toweling robe wrapped over her bathing suit as she drank a cup of coffee in preparation for her swim.

"Hillary! What a surprise!" exclaimed Gee. "I thought you'd be exhausted after your late night." She wrapped an arm around Hillary in a sideways hug as Hillary came to stand at the table.

Hillary smiled down at Gee. "Nope."

"Well, this is good timing, then. I've got something for you. I'll be right back." Gee rose to go upstairs.

Hillary poured herself a big bowl of granola and sat down.

Gee returned momentarily. She was carrying a small paper bag from one of the jewelry stores in town, and she up-ended it over the table and emptied four black velvet jewelry boxes onto a placemat. "I couldn't resist buying you each a little talisman for good luck on your journey." She picked up one of the boxes and opened it. Inside was a small gold ring made up of a pair of hands holding a heart with a crown on it.

"Wow! Thanks, Gee! What is it?" asked Hillary, as she gently lifted the ring from its perch inside the box and turned it this way and that.

"They're called Claddagh rings. They're Irish — symbols of the 'Fishing Kings of Claddagh,' whoever they were! Anyhow, the motto of the ring is 'In love and friendship let us reign,' and the hands symbolize friendship, the crown symbolizes loyalty, and the heart symbolizes love. I thought they'd be good little symbols of your heritage and all that you're seeking." Gee smiled as Hillary pulled hers onto her finger. "By the way, if you wear the heart pointing out, it means you're looking for love, and if it's pointing in, it means your heart is taken. I'm hoping you'll all wear them pointing out! You'd be awfully young to wear it pointing in!" She laughed and gave Hillary's shoulder a squeeze.

"This is so cool, Gee! I'll never take mine off!" Hillary jumped up and gave Gee an enormous hug. "Thank you again."

"My pleasure, dear. Now, I'm off. I'll be back in time to pay Smitty for the boat, though."

"Assuming he shows up," said Hillary wryly as Gee left through the back door.

Across the kitchen, Sheila laughed.

Hillary turned at the sound. "How *do* you know Smitty, anyway, Sheila? We were wondering . . ."

Sheila stopped what she was doing and dried her hands on her apron. She knit her brows together, as if trying to decide what to tell Hillary. Then, with a resigned look on her face, she confessed, "He's my cousin."

"What?!" Hillary was shocked. "How?!"

Sheila smiled. "I somehow thought yas already knew it. Our dads were brothers." Sheila paused. "I'm a Bicket."

Hillary was speechless. "But, but, how . . . ?"

"My ma died when I was sixteen and my da remarried very quickly and produced a new brood, four of 'em, much younger than I. His new wife convinced him to come over here where she had relations and set up a shop instead of fishing for a living, though he always kept a trawler on the side. His wife wanted a fancy life. She always set her sights above her station; the Mac-Carthys always did. Anyways, my da convinced his brother to come along too, and that was Smitty's father. He set up in the boat repair trade here, and my family had the grocers, although it weren't ever really mine, 'cause my stepmother liked to keep it for her boys. You know Robert, Sloan's father, is one of 'em. Sloan's my niece."

Hillary couldn't have been more shocked if Sheila had told her the earth was flat. "So *that's* why you didn't want us starting up the flag planting again?"

"Well, truth be told, yes. It took a long time for all that to settle down, and I got trouble from the Bickets for working over here for the Callahans. Mr. and Mrs. Callahan never minded, 'cause I don't have any stock in what those other Bickets do, and the Callahans knew I was a decent person. But it was awful uncomfortable for me at times."

"I'm so sorry," murmured Hillary. "I had no idea." They were both quiet a moment while everything sank in. Then Hillary took a deep breath. "So would you like us not to do it, after all?" she asked finally.

But Sheila waved her hand dismissively. "No, no. It's a harmless prank, and Mrs. Callahan told me all about your feelings about it. I can understand it. And ya know, that whole branch of the family is no good. Robert, well, he had a chance at being good for a while, but I think he mighta turned out to be the worst. Sloan certainly is."

Hillary smiled. "Yeah, she's a piece of work."

"She gets it from her grandmother, my stepmother. Like I said, the MacCarthys always had airs, thinkin' they were fancier than anyone else. I think my stepmother was competitive with the Callahans from way back, and she got it in her head to one-up them. She'd run them down to her kids, even though Robert and them were all friends with yer dads. She'd say the Callahans were uppity, thought they were so great because they were summer people. All that. And it just kinda trickled down and poisoned the friendships, turned them into a competition."

Hillary was thoughtful. "That name rings a bell . . . Mac-Carthy."

"It's pretty common. Anyhow, it's all water under the bridge. I don't mind if you do it. It'd give me a kick to see you beat that spoiled little Sloan at anything!" Sheila laughed her dry laugh and resumed her picnic making.

"Wow. Can I tell the others?" asked Hillary.

"Ya, sure. It don't bother me none. I just want yas to be safe out there and take care."

"Thanks, Sheila." Impulsively, Hillary crossed the room and gave Sheila a hug. Sheila was embarrassed, but very pleased, and she hugged Hillary back tightly.

After they pulled away, Sheila gave Hillary a swat. "Run along now and get dressed. Smitty'll be here soon and we've got to keep him outta the kitchen or he'll eat us outta house and home."

"Okay!" Hillary left her granola virtually untouched on the table and ran upstairs to get ready and, more importantly, share her news with the others.

Smitty was true to his word again (leaving Hillary to decide once and for all that Sloan was wrong about him). At seven-thirty-three, his contraption began rattling up Gee's driveway. The girls helped carry the boat down to the water and set it afloat; it looked marvelous. He'd cleaned the interior and given it a shiny coat of white paint, and the outside was smooth and repainted, too, save for the shark's mouth on the bow.

The three late sleepers were still reeling in shock from Hillary's retelling of Sheila's confession, but to their credit, they'd each given Sheila a hug and thanked her for her support.

Neeve had laid it on really thickly, announcing that they all still loved her, even though she was a Bicket. But Sheila had taken it well, and was now helping them ferry their things down to the dock for their departure.

With their Claddagh rings and Irish sweaters on (sleeves rolled way up), life vests snugly in place, and everything packed into the miniature boat's interior, the girls were ready to depart. Sheila, Gee, and Smitty gave them a push to get them going, and then stood on the shore, waving at them until they were out of sight. Despite her misgivings of the evening before, Hillary's heart was in her throat. *We're going! We're really going!* she thought excitedly.

Neeve sat, shaking her head as she stared at the retreating figures on the shore. She had finally decided on the zebra-print leggings, with a tube top and three tiny ponytails; topped off with the huge sweater, she looked like a bizarre Pippi Longstocking — half-orphan, half-international pirate of the high seas. "I still can't believe it," she said finally.

"I know," agreed Hillary. She didn't even have to ask what Neeve was talking about. The weirdest part was the MacCarthy aspect. As soon as Hillary had mentioned the name, Phoebe had bolted to her notebook and begun wildly flipping pages.

"Uncanny!" she had breathed, and promptly reminded the others of the ancient battle between the MacCarthy and Callahan clans that they'd read about in Gee's Irish history books. At that moment, the flag planting had taken on a deeper meaning for all of them. It was like they were carrying the torch for some long-dead ancestors. Hillary actually got goose bumps when she thought about it.

Now, Phoebe sat with her notebook in her hand, reviewing the maps and all of their other information. Kate was in the stern of the boat, nervously fingering a flare, as if they might be needing it at any moment.

Hillary smiled at Kate. "Buck up, kiddo! This thing's in top shape, now! If you relax, you'll have more fun."

Kate smiled queasily, but she put down the flare and closed her eyes to face the rapidly warming morning sun. She looked like she was pretending to be somewhere else. But her eyes kept popping open, as if of their own accord. She just couldn't relax.

"Okay, Hillary, you're going to be turning to run between these two islands up here," directed Phoebe knowledgeably. Hillary responded by gently moving the tiller and easing the boat in a new direction. Hillary could hardly wipe the grin off her face, she was so excited to actually be on her way. No one had mentioned Sloan, as if not wanting to jinx the journey, but whenever Hillary thought of her, her stomach clutched and she forced the thought out of her head. She was too happy and having too much fun to let idle worries ruin it. They'd just deal with Sloan if the time arose.

The sailing was going well, as Phoebe directed and Hillary followed. When they were about halfway there, though, Kate, who had been scanning the water and the horizon for any sign of Jaws (or Sloan), suddenly shrieked. "Shark!"

"What?!" yelled Hillary, looking around nervously. A general panic ensued, but Hillary quieted everyone down by yelling "Shut up!" at the top of her lungs.

"Where?" she demanded of Kate.

Kate pointed with a trembling finger off the side of the boat. "Over there. Look! There it is again." And sure enough, they all looked in time to catch a glimpse of a dark gray body with a fin slipping slowly back under the water.

"Oh. My. God," breathed Neeve. "What do we do?"

"Get the radio," Hillary commanded, her eyes never leaving the spot where they'd just seen the fin.

Neeve reached down for the radio, and suddenly there was a big splash, just twenty feet from the boat.

Kate screamed at the top of her lungs and Phoebe looked like she might actually faint. But suddenly, Hillary started to laugh. And laugh.

The others looked at her like she was crazy, until she finally caught her breath enough to gasp, "Dolphin. It's a dolphin. Maybe even two."

"What?" and "Are you sure?" asked the others in tight, panicky voices.

And sure enough, another splash sounded nearby, and the girls turned in time to see the shiny, chubby body dive back down under the water.

"You're right!" exclaimed Neeve gleefully.

"Aren't dolphins scary, too?" asked Kate from where she'd sunk, low in the boat.

"No, silly! They're adorable. And they love people! Besides, didn't you ever hear that a dolphin on your journey is a blessing? It means good luck." Hillary was thrilled. This was the closest she'd ever been to a dolphin in the wild.

"It's true. We see them a lot down in Florida," agreed Phoebe. "They're really cute and nice. You hardly ever see them up around here, but I've heard of them appearing before."

"Well this *is* a good sign, then!" said Neeve definitively.

Kate peeked back over the gunwale of the boat in time to see one of the dolphins do a perfect dive up and out of the water and then back in. And this time she had to laugh, too. "It *is* cute!" she agreed.

After about an hour and a half of sailing, the morning had warmed up and everyone had removed their heavy sweaters and refastened their life jackets. The girls were now in the middle of a cluster of islands that contained Little Gull. Phoebe and Hillary were working hard to stay in the channel and not run aground, as it was now low tide and sandy patches appeared here and there in the waters around the little islands.

"Little Gull is dead ahead," said Phoebe quietly.

Hillary closed her eyes for a moment. No matter what her qualms were about this whole project now, they'd worked so hard toward it that she wanted to savor every aspect of their arrival: the water gently slapping against the boat, gulls crying in the air at a little distance, the sun warming her hair and her shoulders, and the briny, low-tide smell filling her nose. She inhaled a great gulp and opened her eyes.

"That's it! That's it!" Neeve sing-songed. Kate sat way up and craned her neck to get a good look at it, and Hillary just stared.

CHAPTER TWENTY-ONE

Little Gull Island

About the size of a city block, Little Gull Island was low, bumpy, and, of course, gull-shaped. Big, chunky rocks bordered the near side of it, and the rest of it was covered with dune grass and sand. In the island's center was a small rise with some more rocks and a dense tangle of beach plum bushes — almost like an impenetrable little forest. Hillary's palms were actually sweating, and her mind raced with millions of thoughts and questions. *This is it! Is Sloan here? No! Has anyone planted a flag yet? No! What did my dad used to do when he arrived? Was there some sort of a ritual? What should we do first? Oh my gosh! This is it!* And around and around her thoughts wheeled, just like the gulls overhead.

The girls circled the island, searching for a spot to pull in. Finally, on the back side, they found a little pebbly landing and a beach of sorts.

"A little to the left, more, okay . . ." Phoebe had given up her seat, along with her charts, in order to hang over the bow of the boat and direct Hillary visually for the last little bit.

Finally they scraped ashore. "Yes!" Hillary and Phoebe high-fived, and even Kate was happy to be there.

"Whoopee!" called Neeve. "We're here! Yoo-hoo! Sloanie! Watch out, sister! Here we come!" Neeve seemed to have a gift for always saying what everyone was thinking. Luckily, however, there was no sign of Sloan.

Hillary dropped the boat's anchor and lowered the sail, then they all took off their sneakers (with Neeve rolling up her leggings, too) and hopped out. They waded back and forth, from shore to boat, unloading the picnic, towels, and flag onto the tiny fingernail of a beach. Kate quickly radioed Gee back home to tell her they'd made it, and Gee's relief was audible to all of them, even through the crackly connection.

"So, now what do we do?" asked Phoebe, glancing at her watch.

Hillary was giddy with their successful arrival, and hardly knew where to begin. What she really wanted to do was, sort of, hug the island somehow. But she knew the others would drag her home to the loony bin if she even attempted such a thing. So she controlled that impulse and just smiled uncontrollably instead. "You know what? It's funny. All this time, we've been planning and planning, and it was all about getting here! We've never even discussed what to do once we made it!" She laughed. "I mean, besides planting the flag, of course."

The others watched her with smiles on their faces. They were happy to have arrived as well, but everyone really knew this was Hillary's day. They looked at her expectantly for direction.

She clasped her arms together and rocked on her heels; then she peeked over at the watch on Phoebe's wrist. She knew she had to just make a decision. "Um, okay! So. It's ten o'clock now and we need to be heading back by two o'clock at the latest to catch the ingoing tide, right? Why don't we explore a little bit and see if we can figure out where the flag goes? Then we'll plant it, eat, maybe swim, and go?" It was that simple.

Everyone agreed, and they secured their stuff on shore and ambled off, up the island. Neeve was carrying the flagpole in her hand, using it as a walking stick, and the two flags fluttered in the cool breeze like clothes on a line, snapping occasionally when a strong gust of wind blew. Hillary kept checking the surrounding waters to see if there was any sign of Sloan, but so far there was none. She dreaded a run-in with her on this tiny island, and she knew the others felt the same.

The cousins picked their way over the rocks by the shore, then waded up the slight incline, through the sandy dunes.

"I hope we don't get Lyme disease!" shuddered Kate, who was afraid of the ticks in the dunes.

Neeve rolled her eyes and shook her head.

Within half an hour, the girls had looped around the rim of the island. Nothing looked like a likely spot for flag planting, and they were feeling unsure about their next step.

"So, Hills, do you have any idea from what your dad has told you over the years about where they actually planted the thing?" asked Phoebe.

"Well, I know he said they could always see the flag as they were approaching in a boat. Like, they'd know even from a distance if the Bickets had been here," said Hillary. "The only place we haven't really looked is up here, in the center."

"You mean where all those thick beach plum bushes are?" asked Kate.

"Uh-huh. It's gotta be there, in the middle." Hillary desperately hoped that there would be a self-evident flag planting site there. She'd hate to have come all this way and then plant it wrong.

They crabbed their way up the sandy hill and into the scrubby thicket that grew around its center, the highest point. What had looked impenetrable from below, however, was not. They passed easily between the shrubs, with a minimum of scrapes and scratches.

As they climbed the crest, their view improved, and at the top, they had a really good survey of all the little islands around them. The top of the rise was made up of a few huge boulders, no good for flag planting. But in between them, there were deep cracks filled with sand.

"Aha!" said Hillary, peering down. She crawled gingerly on her knees, inspecting the cracks. "It's gotta be here, don't you think?"

The others agreed. "Any special place?" asked Neeve, as she spun the flag in her hands like a majorette in a marching band.

"Ummm . . ." Hillary was inspecting something down in a crack. She stretched her arm down between two boulders and fished around, pulling out a stub of wood. She sat back on her heels and rolled the wood thoughtfully in her hand, as if it were a relic from an ancient world. Could it be a piece of a Bicket flagpole? Or was it a Callahan one? She fervently hoped it was a Callahan one, but either way, this had to be the place. "Here," she breathed quietly. Then she rose from her knees and shouted to the others, even though they were standing right next to her. "Right here! This is it. We'll just jam it right in!"

"Yes!" yelled the others, clustering around the crack.

Suddenly they heard the whine of a boat engine. Hillary's stomach dropped. Sloan! She spun in a circle, looking for the source of the sound, and was relieved to spy a trawler passing a few hundred yards offshore. Phew. It wasn't Sloan.

Now it was time to get down to business.

"So, is there, like, a ceremony, or something? Or do we just plant it?" asked Neeve.

Hillary was feeling expansive, now that they were so close to planting the flag. It didn't have to be she who came up with the actual planting ceremony, as long as they got it planted. She bit her lip thoughtfully. "I think . . . you should just make up something, Neeve, and then we'll plant it. This is kind of your thing, after all," she added generously. Everyone looked at Neeve expectantly.

"Okay," Neeve agreed. Then she closed her eyes to think for a minute.

After a moment, the others glanced at each other, grinning. Leave it to Neeve to really milk it. Finally, with her eyes still closed, she took a deep breath, and began to speak.

"From the ancient battlefields of Ireland, rose the Kings of Munster, the fierce and loyal Callahans," she intoned, in a deep and dramatic voice.

"It sounds like a PBS special," snickered Phoebe under her breath.

"Shh!" commanded Neeve, cracking open one eye to shoot Phoebe a look.

"After many centuries of beating back the MacCarthy clan on the Emerald Isle, the brave Callahans sped to the new world to defeat them on untested soil. And now we, the Queens of Munster, fidus et audax, faithful and bold, stand here today to continue that age-old battle, where good always triumphs over evil and the Callahans always triumph over the MacCarthys (and Bickets). Long may we reign!"

She opened her eyes and looked around at the others. They were laughing and Hillary was shaking her head slowly from side to side. "You are a piece of work, Neeve. You really are."

Neeve flashed her a smile and continued. "Now, we all hold onto the flagpole together . . . no, like this," she commanded. "With your rope bracelet and ring hand." Kate quickly switched her ring from one hand to the other, and then the girls stacked their hands in a row up the pole and shuffled across the rock to the crack. "Now plant it!" shouted Neeve.

The girls jammed the pole into the crack and began wiggling it from side to side to bury it deeper. "Callahan, Callahan," Neeve began to chant, and the others did the same.

"Callahan, Callahan, Callahan . . ." Finally, the pole could go no further. The girls let go and stepped back to admire their handiwork. The pole stood firm and steady in the breeze, and the two flags blew together, past and present, flying in the air.

Hillary felt like she would burst with pride. She almost couldn't believe they'd done it. Her dad would freak out when she showed him, he'd be so surprised. She couldn't wait. "Thanks, you guys," she said shyly. "This is so awesome."

"You're welcome," said Phoebe. "It was fun."

Then Kate shouted, "Yay!" She started clapping and dancing in celebration (*or relief that they were nearly done, more likely,* thought Hillary). The others joined in. They had a big group hug and a moment of silence (at Neeve's suggestion, of course); then they returned to the beach to eat. Hillary lagged behind, though, turning to look at the flag snapping in the breeze. They'd done it! They'd kept the Callahan name alive and flourishing, honoring their ancestors and even impressing themselves. With generosity, enthusiasm, good sportsmanship, manners, and a sense of humor for all!

She laughed out loud and skipped to catch up with the others.

It was now one-fifteen and the girls had to be back on the water by two, in order to catch the tide going in. They began to pack up their picnic and get things in order for the sail home, reapplying sunscreen, putting on life jackets, and generally cleaning up.

By ten of two, the water had risen noticeably up the beach, and the boat, which had been sitting on the rocks, was now drifting freely at anchor in the deeper water offshore. The girls waded out and then swam the last little bit with their assorted gear held aloft out of the water. Kate was not pleased, and by the time she got into the boat she was breathing fast, panicky breaths. Back on board, she shuddered. "I hate swimming in open water," she said unnecessarily.

The others teased her, and Hillary got the sail ready. She took one last backward look at the flag and smiled a huge smile; then she turned the boat and set sail.

The water was definitely running fast; the spring tide was no joke. Even though the wind wasn't that strong, the boat picked up speed quickly, but Hillary was handling it well. But suddenly, there was the unmistakable juddering of a motor in the distance, and a small motorboat quickly appeared on the horizon, off to their left in the next channel.

"Who's this now?" asked Neeve lazily, squinting into the distance. The girls had relaxed after their earlier false alarm, but they'd been too quick. As the boat drew closer, Hillary recognized it from that day on Smitty's dock, and her heart sank like a stone.

It was Sloan.

They were now about a quarter of a mile off from Little

Gull Island, and Sloan was bearing down on it quickly. The Callahans watched as her boat disappeared behind an island to their left, and then reappeared behind them, heading straight for the beach they'd just left. Sloan didn't even look at them.

"No. Way." said Neeve. "It can't be."

Hillary reefed the sail to slow them down, and Kate grabbed the binoculars from her backpack. They floated for a moment, still carried along by the tide, as Sloan went ashore. No one said anything.

After a moment, Kate began giving them the play by play, through the binoculars. "Okay, she's swimming ashore. She's got her flag . . . She's climbing the hill . . . How does she know exactly where to go? . . . NO! She pulled out our flag. She's flipped our flag and she's planting it upside down! And now she's planting hers!"

Hillary's spirits were crushed. After all their hard work, and now this. She'd have nothing to show her dad now.

Neeve started to stand up to get a better look, but Phoebe yanked her back down. "Are you crazy?!" she shouted. "That's all we need! The Bicket flag planted and us capsized out here."

"Sorry," mumbled Neeve. "I just can't stand it."

Kate and Hillary were silent, and then Kate spoke up. "I think we should go back," she said simply.

Hillary was stunned. Kate, of all people!

For a moment, Hillary deliberated. She grabbed Phoebe's arm to look at the time, and the others watched her expectantly. A million thoughts raced through her mind. She thought of

Gee's insistence on only one flag planting. She thought of Tucker's warnings about the spring tide. She thought of the safety of her cousins, in the boat she was captaining. And other things: her parents, happy at a summer party. The fun she'd had all summer, with her cousins and Gee, and the camaraderie — the Callahan-ness of it all. And Sloan staring at them, yes, in envy, Hillary finally decided. But they were so close! Could she possibly let it go? All of their hard work? This was the toughest decision of her life.

Finally, she took a deep breath.

"No," she said. "We can't go back." And slowly, as if in a trance, she trimmed the sail and headed for home.

CHAPTER TWENTY-TWO

Family

Forty-five minutes later, the girls pulled into Gee's dock. The tide had been so strong that their return time had been cut nearly in half. Hillary was wordless on the way home, in a state of shock, almost. She knew she had made the right decision, the safe and smart decision, but it hadn't felt good — especially after all their ups and downs, their diligent labor, and then the giddy euphoria of their success. Everyone was disappointed and all the silliness of earlier had evaporated. Listlessly, they unloaded the boat, and when Gee came running down the hill wreathed in smiles, she was bewildered by the girls' demeanor.

"What happened?" she asked in concern. "Didn't you plant the flag?"

"Yeah," said Hillary, deflated. "But then Sloan came right after us and un-planted it."

"Oh, my dears. I am so sorry. What a shame, after all your hard work." Gee crossed her arms and looked at them sympathetically. "Now you can see why I think that this is not a good game. Someone always feels bad."

"I guess." Neeve shrugged. "I just wish it wasn't us."

They dragged their supplies up to the kitchen and ditched them on the back porch. Everyone wanted to take a quick swim to wash off the salt water and cool down, but it wasn't their usual joyful romp in the pool.

Gee sat on the end of a lounge chair, with her feet primly touching and her knees to the side, like the Catholic schoolgirl she'd once been. "Your parents will be here soon," she said brightly. "They coordinated their flights so they could all get on the same ferry. It's coming in at five-thirty and I thought it would be fun for us to all go meet them. We've got my car, and Sheila's Wagoneer, and Mr. Addison is going to bring his Suburban, too, just to fit them all. I know some of the others are bringing over cars from the mainland. We'll be like a motorcade, coming home!"

"Okay," agreed Phoebe.

"I just wish we had good news for them," added Kate morosely.

Gee thought for a moment. "You know, you don't have to tell them. They don't even know what you were up to. If you'd rather keep it a secret, it's alright with me. I'll just tell Sheila."

Hillary looked up sharply from the pool, where she was sitting on the bottom step, half-submerged. "Yeah. That's a good idea. Let's not tell them. At least, not tonight."

Everyone agreed, and this solution seemed to bring a little relief. The girls decided to discuss their weekend plans instead, and that made them feel slightly better. Besides their parents, all of their other aunts and uncles were coming, and a good bunch of cousins and most of their siblings, both older and younger. They'd been so preoccupied with planting the flag that they'd hardly had time to think about the fun they'd have this weekend.

And yet, Sheila had been running around, scouring bathrooms, stowing groceries and drinks, airing out bedrooms, and generally getting ready to feed and house an army. But she was so used to it, and the house was so accommodating to any number of guests, that the girls had hardly noticed.

After a while, they slipped out of the pool, showered, changed, and got ready to meet the arrivals.

When Hillary first saw her dad stepping off the ferry, she held herself back from running into his arms. She felt the weight of the world on her shoulders, with their unsuccessful flag-planting adventure, and she felt she'd failed him. But his eyes lit up the moment he spied her, and he'd dropped his bags, flung open his arms, and raced toward her. And then she couldn't help but run, too. As she ran, conflicting feelings churned inside her — feelings of failure, doubt, and nervousness, but also feelings of belonging, and the true rightness of that — and she found herself crying with joy, regret, and relief as her dad scooped her into a powerful hug.

The next three hours were a blur of arriving parents and siblings, aunts, uncles and cousins, hugs, reunions, cocktails, showers, and getting dressed for the traditional barbecue buffet dinner on the terrace. Gee's house hadn't felt so lively all summer, despite the girls' energy and presence, and it was fun to have so many people there at once again. The little cousins and siblings — Neeve's sister Ava, Phoebe's sister Melody, and Kate's sister Julie, in particular — darted in and out of the girls' rooms as they got dressed, torturing them, borrowing hair clips, stealing candy, and generally behaving like the lovable nuisances that they were. In the other rooms, the grown-ups and older cousins were busying themselves unpacking and visiting from room to room, and Gee was in her glory — a full house being her favorite thing in the world.

The girls made a quick pit stop in their cousin Maddy's room before dinner. She was seventeen and very stylish and beautiful, so they wanted her to see their outfits and tell them what she thought. She loved everything they were wearing, and helped the girls with their hair. But when she suggested they take off their "junky" rope bracelets, the four protested, so Maddy just rolled her eyes and left it at that. She was too out-numbered to even bother trying to persuade them.

At ten o'clock the next morning, Kate, Neeve, and Phoebe were out at Gee's pool, eating News Co. donuts and hanging out with the rest of the family. Hillary had left a note saying that she'd gone for a run, and they were just waiting for her return so they could head out to the beach for the day. Obviously, a trip to Little Gull Island was no longer in store for them. There wasn't anything there that they would be proud to show the dads.

"Who wants to go get Awful-Awfuls this afternoon?" asked Neeve's dad, Uncle Bill, as he rubbed his hands together in excitement.

"You know I do," agreed Tom, who was Kate's dad. Soon they had a big group that wanted to go — including Kate, Phoebe, and Neeve, plus all of their dads, and Hillary's dad, too. "I know Hillary will come, so count her in," said Kate loyally.

"Alright, then. Three o'clock, we meet at The Dip. Plan your rides now so no one gets left behind," said Uncle Bill. He was the oldest and a natural leader, so he tended to get the plans going.

Hillary showed up soon after that, looking remarkably unsweaty for such a long run. But the others didn't have time to comment on her appearance; Maddy was offering them all a ride to the beach in her cool new SUV, and they had to scramble to get ready.

Everyone wound up going to the beach together, in a fleet of cars filled with rafts, boogie boards, beach chairs, umbrellas, towels, buckets, shovels, and coolers. They installed themselves in their traditional family spot, just to the left of the lifeguard stand, and spent the entire day there, playing, swimming, and buying lunch from The Snack. The four girls laid their towels out together, and indulged Melody, Ava, and Julie by letting them lie nearby, but not too close. Hillary was always nice to them, since she wished she had a little sister of her own, but the others quickly tired of having them around.

"I wonder when we'll see Sloan again," said Phoebe, blowing a lazy bubble with her Bazooka bubble gum, The Snack's trademark free giveaway with every meal. She cracked an eye to peer at Hillary, who had yet to mention yesterday's events. But Hillary's eyes were closed.

"I don't know. If I were her I'd be lying pretty low right now," said Neeve.

"I wish we could go back," said Kate despondently.

"Yeah, but Hillary gave Gee her word we'd only do it that one time," said Neeve.

Hillary was silent.

"Hills, are you asleep?" whispered Kate.

Hillary decided to pretend that she was. She didn't want to get into this conversation right now. There was a pause, then Kate spoke to the others again in a low voice.

"Guys, do you think Hillary's okay? She seems, like, so different today. Distracted, or distant, or something."

"Yeah, I know what you mean," agreed Phoebe in a whisper. "I think she's just really let down about the flag."

"Maybe she misses her mom," added Kate quietly.

"I think we have no idea what she's thinking. And you two should just MYOB," huffed Neeve. Hillary nearly smiled. Neeve had no idea how right she was.

She continued to listen as the subject changed to the family beach picnic for that night. There was a very traditional menu and order to the evening, as it was the yearly celebration of Pops' birthday. Ever since their *parents* were kids, it had been done the same way. Sheila would make the hors d'oeuvres: Mexican layer dip with chips; little chunks of pepperoni and cheddar cheese on toothpicks; fresh vegetables and curry dip; and little cheese puffs of parmesan and mayonnaise broiled on toast. These would all be brought on trays down to the beach, where Cabot's catering would be waiting with a raw bar and a drinks bar already set up. Then the cooks from Cabot's would begin the lobster bake: Small one-pound lobsters known as "chicks" would be steamed with seaweed and then served with corn roasted in the bonfire and cold potato salad. Instead of birthday cake, they'd have blueberry pie and vanilla ice cream. Everyone sat in the sand or on beach chairs to eat, and Gee traditionally invited lots of friends in addition to the family. Tonight, Tucker and Talbot were coming, and the girls were looking forward to introducing their new friends to their parents.

The rest of the afternoon passed lazily, and at quarter to three, the ice-cream worshippers set out for The Dip, while the sun-worshippers stayed on the beach for another hour or two of tanning.

The four girls and their dads piled into the Wagoneer that Sheila had let Hillary's dad have for the day. The girls dusted the sand off their feet and arranged themselves stickily in the hot cargo area for the ride to town. Hillary's dad cranked up the radio, which was playing seventies music, and their dads started singing along loudly and badly, causing the girls to shriek in protest but also to laugh and even sing a little, too.

"God, they are so embarrassing," Neeve said.

Hillary smiled. "Yup."

They parked the car in the town parking lot and strolled around the corner into The Dip. None of their other family members had arrived yet, but as soon as Hillary entered, she had a bad vibe. She looked around the room, and sure enough, there was Sloan — *with her father!* — sitting at a table in the back, eating an ice cream.

Hillary felt like she'd been kicked in the stomach. She quickly nudged Neeve, who turned to look. Neeve's eyes widened, and then Phoebe and Kate noticed what they were looking at. Kate gasped. They looked at their fathers to see if they'd seen the Bickets yet, but no.

"What will they do?" breathed Hillary to Neeve under her breath.

"I don't know," whispered Neeve.

"How about here?" Kate's dad was gesturing to two tables in the front window.

"Yeah. We could pull them together and grab some more seats from the back," agreed Phoebe's dad. He started to walk toward the back, and all the girls took a deep breath.

Suddenly, "Bicket?" he said. *You could have heard a pin drop,* thought Hillary later. All the other dads turned.

The four girls stared at their fathers, trying to read their expressions. Slowly, Phoebe's dad walked toward Sloan's table and stretched his hand out to shake hands with Mr. Bicket. The others followed him; then they, too shook Mr. Bicket's hands.

Hillary's head swam. How could this be? Weren't they sworn enemies? Kate, Phoebe, Neeve, and, most of all, Hillary, were stunned. How could this be? Slowly, inch by inch, the girls drifted to the back of the store.

". . . been so long. God, the times we used to have!" one of them was saying, shaking his head regretfully.

Sloan gave the girls a cool stare. They stared back, then looked in bewilderment at the fathers. There was a pause in the conversation; then Neeve's dad said, "Look, we're sorry about all that old stuff, aren't we, guys?" He looked at his brothers and one by one, they nodded their heads.

"Yes. That turned out to be a bad game," said Kate's dad.

"A real waste," agreed Hillary's dad.

Hillary looked sharply at her father. *Were they talking about planting the flag?* she wondered. *But no, it couldn't be. The Bickets were their enemies and they'd always said so. And now they were apologizing! But why?*

"It's funny you should mention it," Sloan's father began. "Sloan here was just telling me that the younger generation has picked up on it. There's been some new flag planting already this summer."

Hillary's father turned his head swiftly and looked at her searchingly. "Is this true, Hillary? Have you girls started all that old business up again?"

He seemed mad. Hillary hung her head, totally at loose ends. She didn't know what to think anymore. At the beginning of the summer, she had thought that planting the flag was something he'd be proud of; consequently, it became her main goal in life. But in the past week or so, she'd lost her confidence on that score. The momentum of the project had kept her going, but by the time they had set sail yesterday, she'd been secretly questioning her motivations, probing at them delicately like you would a sore tooth. Because ever since she'd arrived, things had been working to change her mind about what it meant to be a Callahan. Her talks with Gee; the nice reputation her family had on the island, evident in the willingness of anyone and everyone to help the four girls; the family resemblance that was so frequently remarked upon; and, ultimately, her realization that she'd been created by two wonderful people in love, who would go on loving her and being a part of each other's lives, no matter what. So, sure, it had been exhilarating to plant the flag, after all, and to clamber on Little Gull Island, and bond with her cousins in silly ways. But she didn't really need all that to feel a part of the Callahan family. She just was.

She looked her father in the eye and said, simply, "Yes. It's true."

Her father was speechless, and Hillary felt her eyes welling with tears. This hadn't been how she'd pictured it.

But Sloan's father interrupted, clearing his throat. "Ahem. I have to say, it's awfully decent, what your girls did. A bunch of bozo guys like us would never have had the sportsmanship to do it."

Hillary looked up, and Kate, Phoebe, and Neeve looked at each other in confusion.

"What's that?" asked Neeve's dad.

"Well, the way they left our flag up and planted theirs next to it. So the two are side by side," Mr. Bicket continued. "Equal."

Now Phoebe, Kate, and Neeve were completely confused. They hadn't done that! What was he talking about? But then they looked at Hillary and saw that her cheeks had begun to redden.

"Hillary?" whispered Neeve. "Do you know anything about this?"

Hillary nodded slowly, her eyes on Sloan. So Sloan had been out to Little Gull today, too! And she'd seen what Hillary had done this morning when she'd snuck out early and hitched a ride from Talbot's dad out to the island.

She'd had the idea to go back and replant the flag when she lay restlessly in bed the night before. And she knew that the good thing to do would be to leave Sloan's flag up, too, so they could end the game and all win in the end. And as the plan had unfolded, early that morning, she'd felt a sense of rightness: of righting the wrongs of generations of Callahans, MacCarthys, and Bickets. With the sun warming and rising in the sky, and the salt spray washing over her, she'd felt like it was the first day of the rest of her life. She was being given a second chance.

Now, in The Dip, Sloan stared back at her, and the others looked between the two of them, back and forth. *So Sloan had left the two flags up,* thought Hillary. She smiled a tiny, tentative smile at Sloan.

And Sloan smiled back!

"It was Hillary!" said Neeve loudly. Everyone turned to listen to her. "We had planted our flag, then Sloan planted hers, and Hillary must've gone back and put the two side by side. Right, Hills?"

Hillary nodded. Mr. Bicket looked at her and said, "That was a really decent thing to do. You're helping to make up for years of ill will between the two families, and years of lost friendship that never should have happened."

Hillary's father looked at her proudly, then threw his arm around her shoulder, crushing her to his side. He kissed the top of her head and said, "I am so proud of you, Hillary Callahan. You give our family a good name."

And Hillary beamed.

CHAPTER TWENTY-THREE

Cousins Forever

$\mathcal{A}$t the party that night, the girls sat in the cooling sand, already full from hors d'oeuvres, and the dinner hadn't even started yet. There would be the town fireworks afterward, when it got dark, and later, if they had the energy, some games or hanging out, back at the house. Right now, though, they were looking around at all of their family members, and gossiping.

"I can't believe how long Ned's hair is, Kate," said Phoebe. "When did that all start? He's quite the Deadhead now."

"I know, it's driving my mom crazy, but I think it looks kinda cute," Kate said. "How about Sarah's tattoo? I thought Gee's eyes were going to pop out of her head when she saw that!"

"I know! It makes me want to get one, though. It looks so cool on her," said Hillary. "Maybe we should all get one of our family crest!"

"Speaking of which, I just have to propose a toast to Hillary. Even though you snuck out on us, it was really cool what you did." Neeve raised a plastic cup of ginger ale at Hillary, and the other two did the same.

Hillary smiled modestly. "I guess I just couldn't leave well enough alone," she said.

"Wasn't it weird the way our dads made up with Mr. Bicket?" asked Kate.

"Yeah, I know, I thought they were enemies and everything," agreed Phoebe.

"It just goes to show you, you think you know how people feel, and then it turns out you have no idea," Kate said sagely.

"I think there was a lot more good than bad between them," said Neeve. "But the bad was so dramatic that it kind of over-shadowed the fun times they'd had. I guess they really were good friends before the flag thing got out of hand."

"I can't believe I ever thought my dad would be proud of me for planting the flag. I must've tuned out the times he said he regretted it, and only paid attention to the fun parts of the stories," Hillary said. "Anyway, I'm glad it turned out alright. And wasn't it weird the way Sloan was almost nice to us?"

"Yeah, it's like she wants to be our friend now," agreed Neeve. "Strange."

But it wasn't that strange, because Hillary had been sensing that for some time now. She'd taken a long walk on Gee's property with her dad, after they'd returned from The Dip. She'd told him all of her feelings about the flag, and the plans she'd had. Her father had been distraught that she'd gone to such lengths to prove she was a Callahan, or to somehow try to win his love. He kept beating himself up about that, but Hillary interrupted him each time. It wasn't his fault, she'd say. It was hers. She had come up with this whole thing and it was over now. She'd learned what she needed to know, and it was something that no one could have told her — she'd just had to find it out for herself. She was a Callahan, through and through. With no need to prove it. She knew she was lucky to have this great family, so it didn't surprise her that Sloan was interested in them.

The walk had ended well. Hillary's dad had reported that he'd had dinner with her mom the night before, just as friends, and they'd had a wonderful time. Hillary didn't get her hopes up for a reunion this time, but she was happy to think that her parents might end up friends. It was enough for now.

Just then, Neeve's dad began tapping on his glass with a plastic fork to get the crowd to quiet down.

"I'd like to propose a toast to my father, whose birthday celebration this is, besides being the Fourth of July. Pops." He lifted his glass to the sky. "Look at what a brood you and mom created. You should be proud. We're sure proud of you and we miss you like heck." Then Bill looked out at the group again. "My brothers and I would also like to propose a special toast to our daughters, Neeve, Hillary, Kate, and Phoebe. You girls have already amazed us this summer. You've stuck together, taken care of each other and our mother, and you set a goal for yourselves that you met. You've also improved the family name and settled a fight that went on for far too long. We can't imagine what you'll do with the rest of your summer! Here's to you." And although most of the guests looked slightly confused, everyone raised their glasses to the girls, who beamed back in happiness.

Shortly thereafter, Talbot and Tucker had wandered in together, and the girls had dragged them from parent to parent, introducing them and telling stories of how nice the boys had been to them this summer. The rest of the party was a blast, and after the amazing town fireworks display, the girls had returned home around ten o'clock.

They were too tired to hang out downstairs, and all the older cousins had taken themselves off to the Witches' Brew, so it was only grown-ups downstairs anyway. They sank wearily onto the beds in Neeve and Kate's room.

"That was a really fun night," said Kate.

"And day," agreed Phoebe.

"Hey!" interrupted Neeve. "You know what I was just thinking about? Our goals!"

"What goals?" asked Phoebe.

"You know, from the cousinship ceremony," prompted Neeve.

Hillary smiled. "Oh yeah. I met mine."

"Really? What was it?" asked Kate, leaning forward eagerly in her chair.

"I'm not telling," said Hillary, and she smiled a secretive smile. "Not now anyway. I'll tell you at the end of the summer, if it's still true. What about you guys?"

"Not yet," admitted Phoebe.

"Sort of," said Neeve.

"Not even close!" moaned Kate.

"Well, we have six more weeks to help each other!" said Hillary.

Just then, there was a soft knock on the door, and Gee came in.

"I just wanted to check on you little chickadees. It can be overwhelming when all of these visitors suddenly arrive and disrupt your peaceful stay here. Are you all having fun?" she asked.

They agreed that they were.

"Good. I just wanted to tell you that I am so proud of each and every one of you. You've behaved like real ladies so far this summer, and true Callahans. Faithful and bold." She winked at them and they grinned back. "And what you did out there on the island —" she looked at Hillary when she said this "— is immeasurably wonderful. What could have been a very divisive event actually became a peaceful, healing thing, and I think that's terrific."

"Thanks," said Hillary softly.

"And I just wanted to make you an offer, since you've been so mature and reliable through your whole visit . . ." Gee paused.

They looked at her expectantly.

"If you feel like fixing up the Dorm to live in, it's yours for the rest of the summer." She smiled.

There was a moment of silence, then the room erupted into roars of excitement.

"I take that as a yes," laughed Gee. "Now I don't want you to think I'm kicking you out. I'd love for you to stay in here, but I thought it might be a fun project for you all. And you're so good at projects, after all. I thought this would give you something to look forward to after everyone leaves."

"And we're not even teenagers!" Phoebe was saying in excitement.

"Actually, you're more mature than some of the teenagers I know," said Gee with a wink. And she left them to celebrate, pulling the door gently closed behind her.

Hillary jumped up and poked her head out the door. "Thanks, Gee," Hillary called.

"You're welcome," came Gee's muffled reply.

"Cousins forever!" Neeve was shouting, as she wheeled around the room with her arm in the air.

"Cousins forever!" Hillary shouted, turning back in from the door.

Turn the page for a sneak peek at

The Callahan Cousins #2
Home Sweet Home

Coming September 2005 from

Little, Brown and Company

*N*eeve Callahan reached the sleeping loft and instantly sneezed from the dust. It was hot up there — the windows hadn't been opened in ages and the heat of the early July afternoon was trapped under the roof. She looked around. Neatly aligned along the wall to her left were four white iron beds, their ticking-striped mattresses stripped of linens. Each bed had a small, white bedside table with a little lamp on it, and opposite the foot of each bed, along the railing that overlooked the living room, was a white wooden dresser. One end of the loft had a tiny bathroom and an even tinier closet, and the other end had a door that opened out onto the back of the Dorm. *Hmm,* she thought. *It would be fun to share a room with everyone all together.* She and Kate currently shared a room, since they'd been the first to arrive, but deep down, Neeve knew she'd have more fun rooming with Hillary or even Phoebe. *Maybe the Dorm would be more fun than the big house!*

"I don't remember this door. What do you think it leads to?" asked Hillary, rattling the handle and then cupping her hands around her eyes to try to peek through its tiny glass window. Because the Dorm backed up to huge clusters of lilac bushes, no one ever went around the back side of it.

Neeve crossed the room to stand beside her. Whatever bravery Hillary possessed or boldness Neeve had was instantly multiplied when they were together. Phoebe and Kate bemoaned the fact that Hillary and Neeve were always dragging them into one preposterous scheme or adventure after another, but Neeve knew that Phoebe secretly loved it. However, Kate was still too much of a baby and it could really get on Neeve's nerves sometimes.

"Well? What is it?" asked Neeve, standing on her tiptoes to get a better look out the dirty window.

"I can't tell yet, shorty!" said Hillary, grinning down at Neeve. "Oof!" Neeve elbowed Hillary swiftly in the ribs. She hated being reminded that she was little.

"Well, we're about to find out!" cried Neeve in glee. "How do we open this thing?"

"Guys," Kate began, "now, Gee didn't mention anything about us going out there . . . It might be dangerous, like a sheer drop to the ground or a hayloft or something. 'Cause I think this used to be a horse barn . . ." Her voice trailed off and she looked at Phoebe for help. Phoebe shrugged. Kate sighed and bit her lip. And Neeve grinned wickedly.

"Does anyone have a barrette or something?" Hillary asked.

"Why?" replied Kate, confused.

"So we can jimmy this door open, Martha Stewart!" cried Neeve.

"Oh, um . . ." Kate searched her hair and then her pockets. "How about a safety pin?"

"Yeah, that might work." Hillary gestured for Kate to bring it to her, then she took the pin from Kate and set to work picking the lock. Surprisingly it took her only a moment, then she stood and threw her weight against the door. The door swung open and Kate gasped and hid her eyes, making Neeve laugh. Kate was probably expecting Hillary to plummet two stories to the ground below, with her long pinkish-yellow braid flying out behind her like a useless parachute. Neeve stumbled out the door after Hillary, yelling "How cool is this!" with a backward glance to check if Kate had opened her eyes. Something about Kate's mother hen routine always made Neeve want to act like a rebellious teenager.

"What's there?" Kate asked pointlessly. Neeve wasn't about to tell her; she'd have to come see for herself.

Once they were all out the door and looking around, even Kate couldn't contain herself. "Wow! This is so cute!" It was a long wooden porch with a little roof protruding out over it to protect it from the elements. Four wicker daybeds — currently draped in plastic to protect them from bad weather — were lined up along the inside wall, just like the beds in the loft inside.

"It's a sleeping porch," said Phoebe, looking around. "They used to use them in the olden days, before air conditioning. Also, for sick people who had tuberculosis and stuff; the fresh air was good for them so they'd have them sleep outside. Like in *Little Women*."

Neeve was distracted because Hillary was already onto the next challenge. She'd crossed the porch in three long strides and begun climbing a ladder that reached up through an opening in the roof.

"This must lead up to that little bell-tower thingy!" she called back over her shoulder.

"Oh, great," whimpered Kate.

They stood quietly as they waited for a report from Hillary. There was a thud and Kate winced, and then Hillary called down to them.

"Guys! This is so cool! You have to check it out! Here. I'll come down so someone else can go up."

Neeve, of course, was next. She scaled the ladder and when she passed through the trapdoor to the tiny landing above, she drew in her breath. She was *on top of* the Dorm — actually inside that tiny lookout tower that they'd been staring at for years. She couldn't believe you could actually go inside it! And the view over the treetops of Gull Island and all across the sound was amazing; Neeve could practically see mainland

Rhode Island from this perch. Wow. She turned in a tight circle — the space in the tower was snug; for one person only — and looked over Gee's entire property, down to the dock, everywhere. She felt like a snail, safe and cozy in her own little house.

If anyone ever wanted to get away from it all, she thought with a peaceful sigh, this would be the place to go. Not that Neeve could relate to that. She brusquely shook her head. She hated being alone. She was a people person.

She climbed back down to the others below.

It was a Callahan family tradition that when you turned twelve, you were allowed to stay at Gee's house for the summer on a "solo" trip, without any parents. Luckily for Neeve, Phoebe, Kate, and Hillary, they'd all turned twelve around the same time, so they got to come to Gull together. They'd already been at Gee's house for several weeks and had just had a week-end visit from their parents that had been lots of fun. But everyone — including other aunts and uncles and several of the twenty-two other grandchildren in the family — had left this afternoon. Hillary's dad returned to Denver; Phoebe's parents headed home to Florida, along with her sisters; Kate's parents went back to Westchester with her brothers and sister, and Neeve's family went with them. Because of her dad's government job, Neeve's family now lived in Singapore. But every summer they made time for at least two weeks' vacation back in the States, traveling around to see friends and family, and then two weeks in Ireland, with her mom's side of the family.

With everyone gone except the four girls, Gee, and Gee's Irish housekeeper Sheila, all was calm and quiet again at Gee's house, which was known as The Sound. In fact, the normally vibrant and athletic Gee had actually gone to take a little nap in her room. And that was when things had finally quieted down enough for them to go check out the Dorm.

Now the girls were back up at Gee's enormous, white-shingled main house, lying on the fluffy pink-and-white-cushioned lounge chairs by the pool and discussing their redecorating plans. Just above them, running along the rear of the house, was a sunsplashed brick terrace, where white iron patio furniture was topped with the same slightly faded pink-and-white-flowered cushions. Neatly ranged about the terraces were huge round planters full of pale pink geraniums. And sprinkled along the tree-ringed perimeter of the back lawn were a slightly overgrown grass tennis court, a trim little herb garden, a trampoline, and a little fingernail of a beach, with a dock and a peak-roofed bathing pavilion. Down to the left, behind the hedge, was the Dorm, the current topic of conversation.

Phoebe had darted up to the room she shared with Hillary in the main house to grab their notebook. (The cousins had recently done a search for an island offshore and they'd used the notebook to keep track of their research and progress.

Now Phoebe had neatly moved ahead to the next tabbed section and titled it "The Dorm.")

"Okay, so what's our plan?" she asked the group.

Kate listed the things she wanted to get: high-gloss white paint for the walls, floors, chests, tables, and lamps; white canvas for slipcovers and curtains; cute fabric for throw pillows; and some burlap or grass-cloth to glue on the coffee table to refinish it.

But now that Neeve was in on the plan, she wanted to put her two cents in, too. The one thing she'd always insisted upon with all of her family's moves was total control when it came to the decorating of her own space. She'd been able to sort of compromise with Kate in their room here in the big house because it was basically already decorated. But if Kate had her way with the Dorm, it would end up looking like it came straight out of a boring old Ralph Lauren ad. Neeve liked Ralph Lauren, but she just wasn't his slave the way Kate was. Anyway, she thought they should have some fun touches, too. They were kids, for Lord's sake, not old married people. She knew she had to step in now, before Kate got too out of hand. So she wracked her brain for fun ideas.

"Hey, uh . . . my old school in Africa had an entire wall in the corridor painted with blackboard paint. It worked just like a regular blackboard, and you could leave messages for your friends between classes and stuff. It was really cool. We should do that."

"Yeah!" agreed Hillary.

Phoebe nodded and added "blackboard paint" to the list.

"But where?" asked Kate. Neeve could tell that Kate's finely honed sense of propriety was offended by the thought of a big black wall in her otherwise white-based color-scheme.

"Well, maybe on the wall where the ladder is? Or even a big square of it, like in a painted frame on the wall?" suggested Neeve.

Kate nodded. "Yes. A small frame would be good."

Small. *Humph!* thought Neeve. *We'll just see about that.*

The talk went on with Neeve suggesting outlandish things — like gluing sequins all over the bathroom mirror frame for a "bling" effect or ordering cheap Chinese slippers over the Internet and then gluing them around the ceiling as a border — and Kate trying to tone her down. But, of course, Hillary and then Phoebe supported Neeve; and Kate, who was the one who would actually know how to make these things happen, started to fume. She sat on her lounge chair, twisting her long, dark hair into bun and then crossing her arms in a huff.

Hillary seemed honestly perplexed by Kate's behavior. What Neeve loved about Hillary was that she was not a girly girl. Hillary didn't play mind games or have big mood swings, so she wasn't usually great at picking up on the other girls' little dramas. It made her very relaxing to be around.

"Katie, are you mad about something?" asked Hillary kindly.

"No," said Kate, looking off into the distance. "Well, maybe."

"What? What is it?" pushed Hillary, truly curious.

"Well, it's just . . ." Kate sniffed and her eyes welled up with tears. "*I'm* supposed to be the crafts one, and the decorating one. And now Neeve has all these fun ideas and you guys are all into her stuff and no one wants to do what I want to do." She quickly wiped at her eyes and stared off at the water, half-embarrassed and half-relieved by her revelation.

"Oh, for goodness' sake!" said Neeve in an impatient but not unkind tone. Sometimes she went too far with bossing Kate around, and then she always regretted it; Kate really was sweet and sensitive and Neeve could forget that when she was annoyed with her. But Kate could just be so babyish! Neeve rose from her lounge chair and went to sit next to Kate. "We can do your stuff! I don't care. Really! I was just trying to think up some fun things — like stuff that would be as fun to *do* as it would be to *look at* after it's done. But we don't *have* to do it."

"But your ideas are actually a lot better than mine," Kate persisted.

Neeve bit her lip thoughtfully. She really wanted the Dorm to be *her* way — she hated to live in a place that wasn't her style — but she'd just have to be patient for now until she could get Kate to come around. "Look, why don't you figure out how to get the basics in good shape. The walls, the floors, and the furniture. Then, if we all agree that we should jazz everything up, we can do that after, alright?"

Kate looked down. "Okay."

"Katie . . . ," singsonged Hillary. "Is it really okay? 'Cause we're not mind readers . . ."

Kate smiled and looked up. "Yeah. It's okay. We could do that."

"Grand," declared Neeve with a relieved sigh. Whenever Neeve's emotions ran high, her Irish accent and her use of Irish words increased. After all, she'd lived there for the first eight years of her life. "What do you say to a snack, then a rummage through the attic?" Neeve proposed, as a change of scenery. Kate loved the attic.

Everyone agreed and after a quick sampling of seven-layer Mexican dip with tortilla chips, reheated Parmesan puffs, and other leftovers from their family beach picnic the night before, they headed up to the third floor of Gee's house.

"It's boiling up here!" cried Hillary, who hated being trapped indoors.

"We don't have to stay long," said Kate comfortingly. She was back to her usual motherly self now that she felt secure again. "We really just need to look around with an eye towards stuff we could use down in the Dorm. Like a stack of old suitcases might make a neat side table in the living room, or something."

Phoebe had gravitated back to the old piles of *Life* magazine that had interested her on previous visits, and Neeve was poking around in the corner, looking at old beach umbrellas that were stored there. Meanwhile, Hillary had spied a big box labeled "Family Photographs" and Neeve watched as she crossed the attic to check it out. Neeve knew that ever since May, when Hillary's parents had finalized their plan to get divorced and her dad had moved out, Hillary had been worried about being cut off from the Callahan side of the family (not that that would *ever* happen, but Neeve could see why she worried about it anyway). Consequently, Hillary was magnetically drawn to old photos and family stories and stuff like that; it was like she needed proof of her position in the family.

Hillary opened the box and called, "Jackpot! Look at all this stuff! We could do a whole family gallery out there, just like Gee has in the back hall upstairs." Gee's simple yet elegant house had fourteen bedrooms and lots of halls, which meant lots of wall space. Gee had been filling the empty space for years with a chronological exhibit of their family photos.

Neeve abandoned her umbrella search and went to look at Hillary's find. There were stacks of framed photos, and Hillary was pulling them out one by one, without even really looking at them. It seemed she just wanted to get a sense of how many were in there. Neeve paused to study a picture of her grandfather, Pops, looking dashing in his Navy uniform. Even though he'd died when she was two, Neeve was glad she'd had the chance to know him.

There were some really funny old photos of Gee, and then some of the girls' four dads with their other brother and their four sisters, all lined up as if for a Christmas photo. Neeve spied another photo of her dad, peeking out from under a pile near Hillary. She reached to pull it out and a couple of other pictures slid to the floor with a clatter.

Hillary jumped.

"Sorry," said Neeve, distractedly glancing down at the 5-by-7-inch photo in her hands.

And then the world stopped.

The photo was of Neeve's father, very young and very dressed up, with a woman in a wedding dress. They were holding hands and cutting a wedding cake together, and people in the background were toasting them with raised champagne glasses.

But the woman was *not* Neeve's mother.

Liz Carey is a former children's book editor. She lives in New York City with her husband and two young sons, and she has twenty-five first cousins of her own.